MY SUMMER ROMANCE

SALLY BRYAN

My Summer Romance

This book is a work of fiction. Events, situations, people and places are all products of the author's imagination. This book contains pornographic scenes and reader discretion is advised.

First Printing, 2014

ISBN-13: 978-1985608610

ISBN-10: 1985608618

CONTENTS

CHAPTER ONE

CHIANTI

I ARRIVED AT THE ENTRANCE TO THE VILLA DI Giordano and peered through the gaps in the huge metal gate. Neat rows of grapevines threaded their way down into the small valley before re-emerging on the hill beyond.

I was about to push the button marked 'Parla' when, of their own accord, the gates began to slowly open outwards from the centre. "Easy." So I grabbed my suitcase and began to make my way up the long dusty track towards the large, imposing villa that dominated the ridge.

It was now evident just how neatly arranged the grapevines were, in perfect straight rows that stretched onwards, only to disappear from sight due to the lay of the land. Men in straw hats and bandanas were pottering through the vines, cutting off stalks and placing bunches of grapes into wheelbarrows. It looked like fun and I was excited to be joining these men in harvesting the grapes.

I was in Italy, Tuscany to be more precise, or Chianti to be exact, for work experience as part of my Italian language degree. My three-year course included a summer working in Italy and I chose to work here because grapes, wine, vineyards and Chianti were what, for me at least, Italy was all about - I was lucky to be here.

I'd met many Italians in England during their work experience and some of the jobs they'd been required to do, for love of the country they were studying, were gut wrenching by comparison. I was a petite, inexperienced twenty year old who'd grown up in a small village and the thought of cleaning wheelie bins, like my new Italian friends back home, made me queasy. I was very much attracted to the idea of manual labour for a summer, just so long as I didn't have to spray down industrial sized waste disposal units. Let's face it, I needed toughening up.

What excited me most about the Giordano vineyard was that they still utilised traditional methods of wine making, the kind of techniques Italians had used before machinery took the romance away from the art. There was a sort of innocence to it, a beauty, and I'd be learning valuable new skills in the meantime, as well as finally being able to speak my chosen language at source. Like I said, it was a dream come true.

The sun baked down on my pale skin as I trundled up the dusty slope toward the villa where a middle-aged man now emerged from a door. He stood slightly hunched, hands clasped at his stomach and even from this distance, his warm smile was a reminder I'd made the right choice. The wheels from my suitcase threw up small dust clouds to my rear, whilst to my fore, the huge villa that was to be my home framed the man who I guessed was the owner of this small, family run vineyard, Signore Giordano.

"Dayna?" He finally asked, approaching to assist with the last few steps. He held out a hand which I took, "I'm Alberto. You found us." He declared in English and a huge smile.

"It's such a wonderful place you have here, I can't wait to have a proper look around," I said, switching to Italian, the relief washing over Alberto's face.

"Ah, I'm so happy your Italian is so good. It will make it easier for us to become great friends." Floppy grey hair encased his features, which seemed to naturally sway back behind the ears. He wore heavy stubble that covered most of his face and possessed an open, friendly nature that would have made him extremely attractive, if only he'd scrub up a little. Alberto, I guessed was in his early fifties.

"Thank you, I've always had an obsession with this country." The heat and exertion had combined to make my forehead prick with sweat and all I wanted was to see my room and take a cool shower.

He noticed and jerked his head towards the door. "Well, what are you waiting for? Come on inside, I'll show you to where you'll be living." He led the way and I duly followed. "You must be tired after your flight, your bus, your walk but I can only permit you to rest after you've taken the grand tour." He was as keen to show me around as I was to see it and I'd happily forego freshening up in the meantime.

The villa was built in the classic Tuscan style with three floors. Great wooden beams supported much of the structure whilst adding a beautiful aesthetic appeal. The floors were all stone tiled, even the upstairs, which gave it a timeless quality.

"For four hundred years, this villa has been in my family and we've been making wine the entire time; through war, revolution and pestilence. We've even survived numerous repossession attempts by bankers and believe me, those sons of whores are worse than any locust plague."

I nodded politely and was happy to see his mood upswing again when we reached a large wall covered with portraits of family members past, which at around the halfway point phased from oil paintings to photographs, from black and white then finally to colour. I paid extra attention to the large framed portrait positioned at the end, which showed a more youthful Alberto with whom I took to be his wife and infant daughter. The happy young family were wearing vintage Italian clothing in the Tuscan style, perhaps in an effort to appear more like their ancestors.

"My beautiful family." He declared with pride. "You'll be meeting my wife as soon as she returns from her errands."

I was about to enquire upon the pretty little girl, who

looked to be maybe seven or eight when Alberto gestured for me to continue up the stairs.

Arriving, we stopped by a door with a plate reading 'Ospiti' and Alberto pushed it open to reveal the guest bedroom. Like much of the villa, the room was modestly decorated, which again harked back to bygone times. It was what I'd wanted, and I'd received it.

"It's wonderful, Alberto." I wheeled my luggage over to the bed and surveyed the large upright mirror that dominated one corner of the room. Opposite was a door to the en suite bathroom and I had a window overlooking the vineyard, bestowing me with a beautiful view of the gentle hills and valleys filled with the vines. Curiosity inclined me to scan the vista for any women my own age, perhaps even the daughter because if I wanted to improve my Italian, it'd be a great help if I were able to make a new friend. There were plenty of rugged looking men brushing and snipping away at branches, some pushing carts along the earth, but there was no sign of any women doing the manual labour. Perhaps she had another job around the vineyard and was not required to carry out the harvesting? I turned back to Alberto, who was standing in the threshold. "There was a young girl in your family portrait..." I trailed off, hoping he'd recognise the question from the inflection of my tone.

Alberto continued to smile, "that would be Alessia, my daughter," and he pulled a photo from his wallet and held it towards me.

I walked over from the window and took the photo, my immediate impression being how beautiful she was.

Perfect symmetrical features and tanned skin so natural to many Italian girls, long brown hair that flowed down the sides of her face to run off the bottom edge of the photo. Her green eyes dominated the face, giving her a serious yet playful look, contradictory as that was, as her smile gave the still image life. If the photo was recent, I'd have put her at the same age as my twenty years.

Returning the photo, I had just one obvious question. "Where is Alessia now?"

Alberto placed the photo back in his wallet and wavered for a second, "she's pursuing a fashion degree in Milano after deciding against working in the family business." He shook his head and sounded resentful. "But as long as she's happy, that's all that matters ... The apple of my eye." It always amazed me how the same sayings we used in English translated directly into Italian, doubtless because they came straight from Shakespeare.

But it was a pity Alessia would not be around and I'd miss the girly chats with my Italian friends back home all the more for it. I reconciled that thought with the reality that my time would fly swiftly by due to the manual labour I'd be occupied with, five days a week, not that I wanted the time to pass fast or anything. During my days off, I fully intended on visiting a host of sites including Firenze, the European Renaissance capital, Siena and San Gimignano, though since there were no females my own age to hang out with, I'd be going solo. Oh well, I was in Italy and intended on enjoying every minute of my time here.

Before leaving, Alberto informed me there'd be an

aperitif in one hour when I could meet his wife Maria and then I was left alone and I gazed at the large bed, wanting so badly to collapse into it.

Throughout the day I'd endured rides on a bus, plane, another bus and finally an arduous walk through steep hills to arrive in the Chianti countryside. My body was sticky from the day's endurance and the shower needed to be paid a visit before anything else.

Facing the large upright mirror, I peeled off my blouse which, having put on in England, was now far too thick for the Italian climate. Next, I kicked off my trainers and jeans, throwing them on the bed.

Turning back to face the mirror momentarily, I was taken by my reflection. I did not consider myself a vain girl by any means, but there was something about staring at yourself in such a large and beautiful mirror. Added to that the natural Tuscan sunlight which poured into the room and together my skin had an ethereal quality to it, unless it was the grime from the days travelling. I had a great figure, I knew that much because of the compliments I received almost every day. I had a lifetime of playing on the fencing team for my county to thank for that. Fencing involved prolonged periods of time standing in semi-crouched positions, which over the years had gifted me with sculpted legs and a butt to go with them. The need to hold heavy fencing blades in front of the body for equally long periods had also gifted me with a toned upper body, as well as matching perky breasts to go with it. I watched them barely quiver as I removed my C cup bra, throwing it over my shoulder onto the bed behind. My blonde hair ran down over my shoulders to rest somewhere against my exposed back. Being blonde, I'd need to pay extra care with the sun, and then I saw how my red forearms had already endured perhaps a little too much of it, having been directly exposed for barely a few minutes. I'd brought a couple bottles of factor 30, which probably wouldn't last long.

The bathtub doubled as a shower and I stepped in, closed the curtain and pulled the lever. The cold water rained down from above, causing a small shock to my system and the day's grime slowly washed away from my body, leaving in its wake goose bumps caused by the chill. I ran both hands over my body in an attempt to generate warmth, feeling my skin's texture with my fingertips. My breasts took the brunt of the cold as the water cascaded over them, my nipples hardening to a point. I cupped my breasts, the large globes more than filling my hands as I took extra care to wash the sweat from beneath.

When I finished, I stepped from the tub and towelled myself, though the warm air coming in through the open windows could have carried out that task with ease.

The aperitif would be in around forty minutes, so I figured I'd have more than enough time to dress in something a little more suitable for the new climate. Then I remembered I'd promised to email my parents and Patrick to let them know I'd arrived safely at the vineyard.

Patrick and I had been dating a little under six months, having met at university after I accidentally wandered into the free weights area of the gym in search of the fencing studio. I'd asked for directions but instead, Patrick took me there himself. Later, I'd caught him snooping through the studio window and after my fencing session, he was still waiting for me to leave. He asked me out there and then and within a few weeks we were a couple.

Although I cared deeply for Patrick, I wasn't in love with him. One thing that set us apart from our friends in relationships was that we hadn't yet had sex. I wasn't too sure why other than it hadn't yet felt right. I wanted my first time to be perfect, and so far, Patrick hadn't created that perfect moment. Some of my friends had fallen in love with their boyfriends after first having sex with them but for me, that felt presumptuous and tacky. What if I ended up giving it away to Patrick and then after everything, I still didn't fall for him? No, I wanted my first time to not only be during the perfect moment but also with the perfect man.

Using my cell phone, I sent a bulk email to mum, dad and Patrick. 'Hi guys, I've arrived safely and will be in touch soon with news and updates.'

CHAPTER TWO

SOLITUDE

THE APERITIF WAS TASTY AND PRESENTED AN intimate opportunity for myself and the Giordano's to become acquainted. Maria brought in several plates of finger foods; thickly sliced bread and olive oil was a staple in Italy and I'd missed it since my last trip. There was also cheese, Parma ham, bowls of olives and sliced tomato with yet more cheese on top. Tomato always tasted fresher out here.

I placed Maria at a few years younger than Alberto. She moved about the living room with a fine lady like grace and it struck me just how much like her daughter she appeared. Not that I'd met Alessia in person and it didn't look like I ever would, but still, my imagination had conjured up an image of the girl. Maria was a beautiful woman and age had not impaired her looks. Her shoulder length brown hair was of a similar shade to her skin and even though her daughter had longer hair, their faces were similar. Her big eyes emitted a warmness I knew would be in sharp contrast to the renowned fiery temper of most Italian women. She was wearing a summer dress that flowed from her shoulders yet still clung to her curves, the hips especially, as though it was short on material.

Maria poured white wine into a large glass carafe, having already set down three glasses and the aroma drifted into my sinuses, filling my world with a pleasant sweet smell. It would be my first taste of the famed Vino di Giordano.

"We're one of the last remaining traditional wine makers in Tuscany." Alberto boasted as he poured the nectar from the carafe into each of our glasses. Of course, I already knew about the vineyard's background, having in my excitement, carried out more than enough research.

"We do everything here just as it was four hundred years ago when Alberto's ancestors began with only a few vines." Maria poured a quantity of olive oil onto a plate and dipped a piece of bread into it. "We're a specialist operation here. We produce less but charge more and we sell our wines around the world." She offered me the plate of bread and I took a few pieces.

I inhaled the wine and couldn't help but hum from the aroma. "I've been looking forward to trying this." I tipped the glass to my mouth and allowed the wine to wash over my palate, the dry fruity taste lighting up my senses. "Oh, it's delicious."

"Now you should eat a small piece of cheese to

contrast the tastes." Alberto placed a small knob of cheese on his tongue.

In the silence, my eyes wandered around the vicinity of the large room and then, for no obvious reason, it occurred to me that these two lovely people had nobody to pass the vineyard down to, at least, no obvious heirs. There was no second child and with Alessia going into a different line of work, I wondered just what would become of this wonderful place and what turmoil lived with the Giordano's for not being able to pass down their legacy? Anyway, it was none of my business and I knew not to ask such questions whilst we were only just beginning our acquaintance.

Alberto suggested that I used the rest of the day to explore the vineyard, as apparently there were lots to see that I wouldn't expect on a typical Tuscan estate.

It was four in the afternoon when I left the villa and made my way down the path through the vines, surrounded by a gazillion grapes and, re-energised from the aperitif, I no longer felt like I needed to collapse on the bed. On the contrary, it was my first day in Chianti and I had the freedom of a world class and fully operational wine making establishment.

Groups of men were working in teams, snipping at small bunches and placing them in tubs which were then packed onto carts. I smiled at them as I walked past and one or two tipped their hats to me. It looked like it wasn't only the vineyard that was traditional but the people as well. This trip would be an experience, already that was proving the case.

Where the vines led into a small valley, a stream cut a meandering path through the vineyard and I reasoned it was probably why this particular location was chosen four hundred years ago to grow grapes. It also created an impossibly beautiful vista for the people who lived and worked here.

I sat on the stream's edge and peered into the water as it flowed by. Removing my sandals, I dipped my feet into the cool water and watched as the fish, startled by my presence soon relaxed and began to circle my feet and nibble at the dry flesh on my toes. I gazed from the crystal clear stream to the distant Tuscan mountains, knowing how lucky I was to be here.

And in the moment, I knew I could stay forever.

Four weeks after arriving at the Villa di Giordano, I'd become accustomed to life harvesting grapes. My primary task was searching for ripe bunches on the vines, cutting them from the branch and placing them in tubs. When the tubs were filled, I piled them in the cart. When the cart was full, I wheeled it with the help of one of the other workers, towards the winery.

I was keen to learn about the rest of the process but actually making the wine far surpassed my pay grade. For the most part, the days past fast enough, even though they were entirely monotonous. Lugging around heavy containers all day proved hard work and I could begin to feel the muscle tone in my arms further improving from the effort. Even my skin became accustomed to the hot sun as, throughout the course of the month, I began to use ever less sunscreen until the time came when I didn't need any at all and I possessed a healthy golden complexion.

Though the truth was that I longed for some company, any company. The guys I worked with were pleasant characters but were mainly in their fifties or sixties, which meant they were older than Alberto. In addition, the majority of them had migrated up from the south, one or two from North Africa, and spoke with a southern Italian dialect I was unfamiliar with or with a different language entirely. Alberto and Maria understood them mostly but since I was studying generic Italian, I struggled just as they struggled to understand me.

Alberto often visited the workers among the vines and would check to see how I was doing and make small talk. Though being more involved in the winery and having such a heavy workload, I rarely saw him even in the evenings.

At least, at first, the evenings were more tolerable as Maria and I would often chat over wine about Italy, food and music. But her job involved long periods away from the vineyard, travelling north to find new buyers. She'd return at weekends with new contracts from restaurants who'd agreed to stock Vino di Giordano but then, as soon as Monday rolled around she'd be gone again and wouldn't return until late Friday.

It soon became apparent, as I pottered about the villa,

that I had free run of the place. Ordinarily, I'd be ecstatic, a palace for myself. If only I had some company.

Even the weekends proved anticlimactic, as I failed to make use of my time as I'd hoped. It was as though I'd fallen into a rut, a negative spiral of boredom, defeatism and dare I say it, even depression. Only during my first weekend here had I visited the nearby town of Poggibonsi and not once had I ventured beyond to places of interest such as Firenze, Sienna or Monteriggioni. The fact we were out in the countryside hardly helped and public transport around here was non-existent. I'd been offered the use of a vehicle but I'd never before driven on the right and was too nervous about damaging my host's car.

It was the beginning of my fifth week, having only completed a third of my time in Chianti. At five o' clock and tired, I wheeled the cart up towards the winery and parked it beside the one I'd wheeled in earlier in the day. Another full evening of solitude awaited me and for whatever reason, I'd just had enough.

I flipped open my laptop and sent an email to Patrick. 'Hi babe, sorry I've not been in touch lately. I've not been having the greatest of times here, I'm missing you lots and thinking of returning home.'

I stared blankly at the screen, wondering if I meant the words I'd written. Then I clicked send.

Shutting the laptop screen, I collapsed back onto the bed and laid still for several minutes, studying the swirly patterns on the ceiling. What else was there to do? There had to be something, but what?

I shambled downstairs and made my way through the

stone tiled hallway towards the living room and the heavy oaken door with wrought iron ring handle at the far end. It was a room I'd been in only a couple of times before. It contained a billiard table, antique chess set and a large storage chest of which I had no idea what was kept within. Since the room appeared to be some sort of a boy's games room, or man den, I hoped the chest might contain something of interest, something to liven up what I'd decided would be my final Monday here.

The key to the chest was in the lock and I turned it, feeling the click. The lid was heavy but nothing compared to the carts I'd been pulling and I pushed it open and peered inside.

Wow.

It truly was a boy's games room.

The chest contained a selection of radio controlled cars, boat and even a plane, an old retro Nintendo from the days before I was born along with a huge array of cartridge games stacked neatly to the side. I leaned into the chest and began to rummage further through the goodies, regretting not scouting this lot out weeks ago. I shifted aside a pair of rollerblades, obviously too large for my little feet and found what I knew I'd be playing with tonight. For whatever silly reason, the Scalextric set was kept right at the very bottom. I'd played on my father's Scalextric as a girl and used to delight in beating him and I felt a beautiful wave of nostalgia wash over me as I envisioned the hours of entertainment ahead. I shifted more stuff aside as my fingers grafted and clawed for the box, and just as I grabbed a hold of it...

"Who are you and what are you doing in my house?" A shrill feminine voice called from behind, aimed directly at my rear end which was pointing straight at the voice.

I yanked the box free, straightened and turned around, wide eyed.

A young woman was standing in the room's entrance, one hand hidden behind the heavy oak door, the other touching her collar bone whilst her feet were turned towards the escape route in flight preparation. Yet in stark contradiction, she was standing bolt upright, in apparent opposition to me, almost like she was unsettled but didn't want to show it, I was only a young woman myself, after all, and worried she might lurch forward with whatever might be held in her concealed hand. She wore grey jogging bottoms and trainers along with a sleeveless sports vest and I wondered if she'd returned from a run because there were small beads of sweat pricking at her forehead. Surely I wasn't that terrifying?

A few seconds was all she needed to see I was no threat to her, having been scared shitless myself, and whilst she awaited an answer, my thoughts turning to mush, she took a single step within, no weapon, and placed her hands on her hips, showcasing an athletic figure and toned arms I had no desire to grapple with. Her dark hair was tied back into a ponytail and hung down past her bare shoulders. I knew exactly who the girl was, since she looked almost identical to her beautiful mother with big piercing green eyes that were now staring holes through me.

"I'll ask you one last time before I call the police." She fired off in quick Italian and for a moment I needed to think about the translation. "Who are you? And what are you doing stealing my family's possessions?"

I lowered my brow and held out my palms as something rattled from within the box. "I'm sorry. I was just looking for something to do." My voice sounded embarrassingly high pitched.

She didn't budge and looked formidable. "Why? Who are you?" If she'd looked afraid before, she most certainly didn't anymore and knew she had me like a mouse caught by a cat.

"I work here. I'm on work experience. I've been here for a month. I live upstairs in the guest bedroom. I'm not stealing anything." I watched as she trod further into the room, her feet pointing straight at me. "I'm sorry, I just wanted something to do." I said with a little more confidence.

"Your accent ... you're not from Italy?"

"Nuh uh," I shook my head, "Like I said, I've been living here. I wasn't stealing anything. Your father's name's Alberto, your mother's called Maria."

She breathed and her face softened, her expression still anything but friendly, but at least, I was certain, she'd no longer call the police on me, and I doubted very much she'd jump me either. Being attacked by a fiery Italian was the last thing I needed, especially considering she was the daughter of my host. Though I'd have given anything for just a small indication of friendliness from the girl, if only to prevent my heart from bursting through my chest as the adrenaline continued to pump through my body.

"The Scalextric," she nodded at the box I was still holding, "I broke that last summer."

"What?"

"I broke the stupid thing last summer ... accidentally of course ... but it doesn't work anymore and I'd much prefer it if my dad never found out." The tiniest hint of a smirk grew on her face.

I exhaled deeply. "It's our little secret then. I won't tell."

"Good." The smirk curled into a full on smile, which finally relieved the tension.

"But you have to promise not to beat me up because if you beat me up then I'll tell your dad you broke the Scalextric." I dumped the box back in the chest and made a sad expression. "I really wanted to play on that." I knew I was jumping the gun by being playful so soon after we'd both undergone a threatening experience but my mind needed to make compensations.

"We can play on the Nintendo instead." Forgetting all caution, she made her way past me and went to the chest as the sweet smell of spice mixed with jogging sweat pervaded my small personal space. "And I promise not to beat you up."

She bent over and leaned into the chest and it was hard not to notice the impressive feminine curves of her slender body. Her slim waist gave way to wide hips, gifting her with an impossible hourglass figure. She was her mother's daughter, that much was true.

My heart rate increased yet further and for whatever strange reason my right hand was trembling but I knew it to be the after effects of being made to feel like a burglar caught in the act. I balled my fingers into a fist, stopping the sensation as she pulled out the Nintendo.

As she stood up straight, her bare arm brushed against my breast. Had I been stood too close? I couldn't be sure. It was she who'd approached a little too close and I was pretty certain all I'd done was remain rooted to the spot. Anyway, why was I thinking such stupid, meaningless and irrelevant thoughts, I wondered, as my nipple still tingled from the contact of her arm. I had small nipples but they always stood to a point when stimulated, I was a freak like that, and I prayed my breast would not make a show of me through the thin layer of flowery fabric which had divided our flesh.

She held the Nintendo and a couple of games cartridges under her left arm as she extended her right hand towards me. "I'm Alessia, by the way."

"I know." I accepted her hand and was surprised by the firmness of her grip and how it contrasted with the softness of her skin, except for the faint roughness of callouses at the base of her fingers, evidence perhaps that she lifted weights. For sure that would have explained her firm handshake and subtle appearance of feminine deltoids, but then again, I often suffered from callouses from hours holding a fencing blade, not to mention pulling carts.

Again, my thoughts went fuzzy as I became aware that several seconds had transpired and not only had I not told Alessia *my* name, but I found my thumb to be lightly stroking the area of skin between her thumb and forefinger.

"I'm Dayna," I blurted out, "and it's nice to finally meet you."

She released my hand and because my nipple was still irritating me by tingling, I was filled with a sense of self-consciousness and the need to glance down, just to be sure my one area of insecurity wasn't causing a potentially embarrassing problem. The pleasantries were over but she was still standing close, too close, like she had no concept of personal space, or maybe she was just being friendly?

"Well then Dayna, let's set this thing up, I'm best in my family at Bubble Bobble." She turned and stepped out the room as my eyes were drawn to where her slim waist met her broad thighs.

Why was my knee shaking? Was my body still recovering from the surprise of our initial meeting or was it something else? I had indeed been shocked out of my skin when she startled me, so yes, it had to be that.

After all, if I was attracted to Alessia, then that would mean I was a lesbian, and I was not a lesbian. I had a boyfriend back in England, who only moments before, I'd emailed to tell I was returning home.

As I followed Alessia into the living room, I glanced down at my breasts.

To where my nipples, stiff and pointed, were thrust hard and visible through my summer dress.

CHAPTER THREE

ALESSIA

WHILST ALESSIA WAS SETTING UP THE GAMES console, I slipped to the bathroom to sort myself out, tying my hair into a rather unflattering ponytail and intentionally leaving errant strands over my face. Seriously, of all the afflictions to be born with ... I remained in the small, boring, room until I was satisfied my nipples would not expose me, or themselves. I also gave myself a stern talking to, reminding myself I was in a relationship with a guy I loved, even if that was stretching the truth a bit.

When I returned to the room, a bottle of chilled wine was positioned on the table along with two glasses.

"Merely to become acquainted." She said, filling the glasses almost to the very top.

I sat down after her and was careful to leave a large space between us, but not so large it would look like I was deliberately creating a void. It was nearly seven in the evening and with the last of the day's remnants still filling the sky with light, Alessia had closed the blinds so that only a fraction of light shone into the room. The effect gave a radiant quality to her skin and further brought out her bright eyes.

"Well, it would be rude to play an old classic without doing it properly." I said, more out of politeness than anything else. The thought of drinking wine right now made me uncomfortable. It wasn't that I didn't know her, after all, what better way of getting to know a person other than by sharing a nice bottle of wine? No, it was more that considering our initial encounter, which I was still shaken by, her sudden change in mood, confidence and demeanour was a little strange for this English country girl. My head was already swirling and I didn't fancy adding alcohol to the mix, even if it was Vino di Giordano, which made saying no all the difficult.

Alessia handed me a glass. "There you go, Dayna." She was deliberate with my name, drawing it out and softening her tone. Then she lifted her bum from the couch and halved the gap between us in one fluid sidewards motion.

My fingers tightened around the glass as I contemplated the likelihood of possessing the stealth to shuffle further away without her noticing. "Is it just the two of us here tonight?"

"Huh?" She was leaning forwards to take her glass from the table, her tight tank top not preventing her breasts from leading the way, bra strap bulging through the back of the stretchy grey material. She took a small, lady sized sip before returning the glass and sinking back into the brown leather to return parallel with me.

"Are your parents around tonight?" I asked in a different way, leaning subtly to the side.

"Yup." She said nonchalantly, more interested in starting the game as the music came to life. "At least, Dad is. He's cooking dinner."

It was a relief. "And Maria?"

"Mum? Beh, she's up north somewhere ... don't know where."

Well, since she didn't give two hoots for the answer, I grabbed the control pad and began pressing the buttons as some little green dinosaur shot things from its mouth at what looked to be tin cans but were probably some sort of monster. The game was obviously very old and the graphics were a throwback to the early days of gaming, though it was all new and intriguing to me. For whatever reason, my little green dinosaur wouldn't respond to my commands and I thought about asking Alessia if the control pad was broken, she had previous, after all. The theme tune was more than just a little catchy and I feared it'd be in my head all night long. But seriously, if Alessia had seen Alberto beforehand then why had she not been told there was a girl her own age sharing the house? Had it not been suggested she come find me, talk to me, make me feel welcome? Had she been playing a game on me before? Did she usually acquaint herself with people by causing an argument and a scene? No, of course not, because that would be absurd and my mind continued throwing up paranoid thoughts whilst her hand made constant tapping sounds on the control.

"Aren't you touching your wine?" She turned her head to me for the briefest of seconds before returning to pay attention to the screen.

"Um, I don't think this controller is working. This green dino thing isn't moving where it's supposed to."

And then Alessia snorted so hard that she needed to clasp a hand over her nose to cover whatever the heck had just shot out of it. "Oh my God, that's too funny." She ran to the cabinet, pulled out some tissues and blew her nose.

"What? What did I say?" I was genuinely confused by whatever had caused her to laugh so hard she caused herself a near accident.

Alessia dabbed her nose in front of the mirror and threw the tissue in a waste paper basket. "You really shouldn't make me laugh like that, I tasted wine." She sat back down, again a little closer than what made me comfortable and turned to face me.

"Will you let me in on this joke or what?" Now I felt even more self-conscious than before.

She placed her hand on my bare arm, cold from the wine glass and I felt a small shiver run down my back. "Oh Dayna, you're the blue dinosaur. I'm the green one." She grinned, her white teeth contrasting against her tanned skin and for the first time, I could truly appreciate just how beautiful she was, so much so that it made me wonder if it was the source of my present insecurities.

She rubbed my arm and the grin morphed to yet

more laughter and in the moment, I saw the funny side too, how could I not? And so I laughed. I laughed hard and much of the tension I'd felt dissipated. It felt good to laugh, perhaps I'd been silly and should learn to be less uptight and paranoid, more accepting and definitely more chilled out.

"Well ... that totally explains why my green ... dinosaur wasn't responding to my ... commands." It took me a while to say and after all that I felt looser and reached forward for the wine, taking a large sip. It went to my head but in a good way.

Alessia gave my arm a final rub, picked up her controller and paused the game, bringing the catchy tune to a stop. She turned back to face me and looked into my eyes. "You are silly, Dayna." She again drew out my name as she accented the 'ay' and reached for my forehead. Instinctively, I flinched away but then the errant strands of hair that were falling over my eyes were swept aside. "That was annoying me." She laughed again and I rolled my eyes.

I realised that this was most likely Alessia's nature, odd as it was to me. Confrontations with people she didn't know, the invasion of people's personal space, breaking Scalextric sets, playing video games from years ago and shooting snot from her nose. She was a tomboy of the most obvious sort. Most girls I knew, particularly the Italians back home, were all girly girls but Alessia was something different and it'd just require some getting used to. This was why I'd felt nervous and uncertain but I'd now found the root cause and wouldn't let it affect me anymore. What's more, I was now actually quite intrigued by this girl.

She continued to study me as a silence persisted between us, which really should have felt uncomfortable but for whatever reason, did not. She truly did have the most flawless skin, the benefits of a lifetime living in a hot climate with fresh country air.

Her head tilted to one side. "You really are tense aren't you? Here, let me..." she jumped up and I leant forward as she walked around the back of the couch and disappeared from view. "Here, now, let's try this." And suddenly two hands were on my shoulders and I was pulled back against the couch.

"Oh, my..." I uttered, my alarm dissipating, as she began working over my neck and shoulders with her palms and fingers, the feeling indescribable, like the tension was evaporating with each and every movement of her hands. Weeks of manual labour, harvesting grapes, carrying heavy boxes and pushing carts had taken their toll in ways I hadn't realised and now her touch was releasing all my pent up stress.

"You really are all knotted up. You see? I knew it. You should learn to relax more." Her upper body was visible as a reflection in the TV screen as she continued working over my shoulders and she appeared to be watching my reflection in the same.

I prayed she wouldn't stop and I closed my eyes and dropped my head back to nestle against her wrists. Heaven. But it wasn't to last.

"Ikari Warriors!" She exclaimed and then her hands

were off me as my neck begged for more and she was dashing back in front and over to the Nintendo. The screen went fuzzy as she turned off the games console and exchanged cartridges before turning it back on again. The TV blared out a new theme tune, which I didn't think sounded anywhere near as catchy as the first.

I brought my head, which had been dumped on the leather headrest, back to a level posture just as Alessia sank back into the couch, throwing me a control pad. Bizarrely, she was now sitting back in her original position with a large gap between us, which I thought could possibly have been even wider than before.

The words that came to mind were; hyperactive, ADHD, scatty and possibly even a good sort of loopy. Too much wine over time perhaps?

"Don't forget, you're the red warrior." She said, barely disguising the patronising tone.

"Um, thanks."

Confused - That was the best way of describing things. What had just happened? Why was she hot one minute then cold the next? Either the girl was, after all, playing some kind of game on me, or she had a low attention span and was unable to stay rooted to any one spot for more than a minute.

And I wasn't sure why but not knowing drove me crazy.

"It's called pappardelle." Alberto said as he tipped

a portion of the thickest spaghetti I'd ever seen onto my plate, which was then followed by a meaty sauce. "The sauce contains wild boar and tomatoes grown on the estate ... fresh." He said as though the final word made all the difference in the world.

"Dad makes the best pappardelle." Alessia added and smiled at her father.

The smell had been drifting through the house as we were playing Ikari Warriors, in silence, and in truth, I just couldn't wait to get the damn game over with so I could eat. In fact, Alessia's comment about the pappardelle was the first I'd heard her speak since giving me that massage.

Her phone vibrated against the table and Alberto frowned as she put down her fork to pick up the phone, fired out a rapid message and returned to her meal.

We'd brought the remainder of our wine to the table and now Alberto poured more into our glasses. "When in Rome."

I plucked a piece of bread from the plate in the centre. If the pappardelle didn't soak up the alcohol then the bread sure would.

"So, Dayna, you're still having fun here, I take it?" Alberto asked as he ravelled a strand of the obscenely thick spaghetti around his fork. "Long days in the hot Tuscan sun are not exhausting you too much, I hope?"

I hesitated before answering. "I am still enjoying myself, thanks." The tone of my voice may have had a touch of unhappiness to it and from the look on his face, he sensed something was not quite right.

Alberto was about to say something when again,

Alessia's phone vibrated and instead he threw up his hands and leaned back in his seat.

Alessia fired off another message. "The English are in great need of vitamin D." She said, still staring at her phone, though the comment was directed not at me but her dad. Her body was gently swaying side to side, like she was swinging her legs to and fro beneath the table.

And in any case, I still hadn't told her I was English, so how did she know? Had she been told by her dad that an English girl was staying here? Or was it simply obvious from the conversation we'd had that I was from England? It wasn't an absurd assumption. More questions flew around my head and it was all because this girl had somehow managed to get under my skin.

"You've certainly browned a shade or two." Alberto said before shovelling more pappardelle down his mouth, evidently having neglected what he was about to say before.

The work here at the Villa di Giordano was enjoyable, I had no problem with that side of things. The main problem this past month had been that I was lonely. But now with Alessia here I'd at least have someone to talk to in the evenings, someone my own age, even if from what little I knew, she hardly acted it. If I could learn to live with her personality swings then the remainder of my time here, two months, might be more fun. It all depended on whether she'd be around whilst I was, or if she'd breeze off on the next whim. Rather than hope that particular topic came up naturally in conversation at dinner, I decided to just ask her straight up myself.

"So, Alessia, I hear you're studying in Milano, how long are you visiting home for?" I picked up another piece of bread and began to layer it with butter.

Alberto turned to face his daughter and it occurred to me I'd asked the very question he'd wanted to ask himself

Alessia's phone vibrated again and Alberto thumped the table.

"Will you tell Marco to stop texting when we're eating." He threw up his arms. "My parents would have thrashed me but alas, God gave me a daughter." It was the first time I'd heard Alberto raise his voice, or at least it was his attempt at berating his wayward daughter.

But more to the bloody point – Who the heck was Marco? Did Alessia have a boyfriend? If so then why was she playing games with me? Why had she borderline seduced me before turning cold again? Assuming, of course, that's what it was, there was simply no way of knowing.

"They're not all from Marco." Alessia chided, casting me a cheeky sideward glance.

Then I felt the contact beneath the table, which had to have been her foot. At first, it was a slight brush, which I assumed to be a consequence of her swinging her feet a little too wildly. The second contact came a few seconds later, a slow rub up my calf with her toes and, naive I may sometimes be, but that can't have been accidental. All this whilst Alessia simply continued to text and as I raised a questioning eyebrow at her, she did not so much as look up.

I pulled my seat back a few inches, cringed at the

sound of wood on stone and further tucked my legs in beneath my chair, out of the range of Alessia's prying feet. I considered dropping Patrick's name into the conversation, as I had with Alberto and Maria when they'd asked about my domestic situation, if only to imply to this girl that I had a boyfriend back home and more to the point, that I was straight. But I dismissed that idea as soon as it came because it was wrong, as well as unnecessary, to bring Patrick into whatever silly games some girl I'd only just met might have been playing.

A static sound omitted from the security panel and then came a scratchy voice. "Hi, Alessia? It's Marco."

"He's here." She pitched back her seat and beamed as she hurried to press the button.

Alberto exhaled loudly and rubbed at his bristles. "Sometimes ... What I wouldn't have given for a son instead. Maybe it would have been possible to get through *one* meal without the town calling in. Or at least if she'd have been blessed with my looks instead of her mother's."

I laughed into my pasta, curious to see this Marco.

It took a few minutes to hear the door opening, which was followed by the thud of it closing and I tried to feign disinterest by winding an extra slippery piece of pappardelle around my fork. For whatever reason, I could sense Alessia paying close attention to me.

"Ciao Bella," came the clichéd greeting from a masculine voice to my rear. Then Marco walked around the table to Alessia and stooped to kiss her on the cheek.

She, in turn, threw her arms over his shoulders into a strong embrace.

Marco straightened, turned to Alberto and shook his hand. "Alberto, come stai?" Finally, he noticed me and his smile lifted yet further. "And Signora, who are you?" He moved around the table and took my hand, kissing the area of skin just above the knuckles. It really was difficult not to be charmed by such behaviour.

"Hello, I'm Dayna." I said, probably blushing, and noticed the brief cold stare from Alessia.

Alberto set a plate out for Marco and scooped him a generous portion of pappardelle. Marco then took it upon himself to fill everybody's wine glasses, even though mine was already close to the brim.

He had kind blue eyes and long brown hair pulled into a bundle at the back of his head, a look that would not suit many people, yet this man pulled it off with ease. His finely trimmed beard gave an extra element to his face, which had an overall warm and friendly quality to it. His nature was relaxed and easy, or at least it was around the Giordano family and I wondered, along with other questions, if he was a neighbour.

"They're old friends from childhood." Alberto spookily answered my thoughts, gesturing with his head toward the two. Though from how Marco was sitting with Alessia's hand in his lap, it was obvious they were, or at least had been more than friends. I certainly wasn't that close with any of my male friends.

"Alessia's the love of my life." Marco declared, though I knew this was how many Italian men were around women, their mothers even, and that such statements in Italy meant something completely different to how they would back in England.

"What do you do, Marco?" I asked.

"I show tourists around the beautiful city of Firenze."

"Ah, so if I need to know the best places to see, I must come straight to you?"

He squared his shoulders to face me and leaned forward. "Signora, I could show you the most beautiful wonders Firenze has to offer. I'd be happy to show you around any time you wish."

For the briefest of flashes, Alessia's eyes widened and I thought I saw her shift ever so slightly in her seat. She couldn't have been jealous. Of that? Why? There was no need. My interpretation was that Marco was merely stating his knowledge of the city, followed by a polite conversational offer to show me around. And as everyone knows, such offers are never taken up.

"That would be a great idea, Marco, and if you'd like to continue feasting at this house, you will be held to it." Alberto interceded with a stern expression. "The girl has worked hard for over a month and deserves to see more of Tuscany than this God forsaken vineyard."

Marco pulled his seat closer and spoke with animation. "I do not joke about such things and of course, it would be my pleasure." His handsome grin further broadened. "We can go tomorrow."

I scratched my cheek. "It's a wonderful offer and I'd truly love to see Firenze but I have to work tomorrow."

"Nonsense." Alberto slammed his hand into the

table. "You now have tomorrow off and that's all there is to it." He stood, taking his wine and left without even looking back.

Marco laughed. "Looks like you've been told and so that's it, settled."

Alessia sipped her wine, her glass less full than anyone else's and she began to look increasingly uncomfortable as the conversation progressed, as Marco turned further away from her and closer to me, which I had to admit, gave me a small amount of sadistic pleasure. "Ok, so what time are we leaving?" She asked, taking Marco's attention by grabbing his hand and bringing it into her lap.

"Um, the earlier the better." He replied, pulling his hand back and looking at me. "There's so much to see. We can skip the line at the Uffizi as well as the Academia and I can get us inside gratis Signora. I'm friends with the manager of a restaurant that overlooks the Duomo, so we'll have magnificent tables there. And I have surprises waiting too."

I was so excited. I'd always wanted to visit the Renaissance capital and now I'd have my own tour guide too, as well as free entrance to the best attractions. How could a girl complain? It would also be a chance to discover just what Alessia was about, to try figure her out and satisfy my curiosity.

Marco lit the candles that were on the table and we drank wine whilst he spoke with such engaging excitement of the city and his promises for the next day. It wasn't often you met someone so passionate about what they did and it was endearing. Throughout, he and Alessia held hands and every time he let go in order to gesticulate, she would always grab it back, pulling it into her lap. Mostly, she tried doing it subtly, but once or twice failed miserably and it appeared more like overcompensation on her part, almost like she was making a statement by keeping him close – and away from me. I wasn't a complete idiot when it came to these things, I was a woman after all, and knew there were motives behind Alessia's possessiveness. Either she was warning me off Marco or was insecure about something else – And I guessed that something else was me. I wanted to be her friend, I knew that much, because that was the type of person I was and it would definitely make the rest of my time here more enjoyable. I most certainly did not wish to make enemies in the meantime.

Marco leaned forwards. "Do you have a boyfriend back home?" You had to hand it to them, these Italian men were straight to the point and Alessia caught my eye from across the candles and wine.

I'd tried keeping Patrick out of it, but since I was asked the question first, I would not lie either. However, I did give it some thought and realised the answer I was about to give would be just as much for Alessia's benefit as for Marco. More importantly, and for whatever reason I did not know, I wanted to get a reaction from Alessia, maybe even make her jealous. The scary thing was that I didn't know why.

"Yes," I confirmed, "he's called Patrick and we've been seeing each other for around six or seven months." I spoke to Marco but attempted to concentrate on Alessia's reaction. I got nothing, she'd make an excellent poker player.

"Well, I'd say this Patrick is a lucky man." Marco said, slapping the table to emphasise his point.

And this prompted Alessia to throw his hands back into his lap with a sudden and unexpected fury. She then stood with the scrape of wood on stone before ramming the chair under the table and storming from the room. Poker player? Perhaps not.

Marco tipped back in his chair, hands clasped behind his head. "Ouch, something I said?"

CHAPTER FOUR

FIRENZE

I woke extra early. So early, in fact, that I tried returning to sleep. It turned out to be an exercise in futility and I couldn't figure out if it was due to the excitement of the coming day or because of Alessia and her histrionics.

Finally, at six in the morning, I threw back the covers and staggered toward the shower. I found myself thinking about Marco as the warm water cascaded down upon me. He was devilishly attractive in the stereotypical Italian sense and I was intrigued by his natural charm. However, as my hands ran down my body toward my wet folds, what alarmed me was that it was not Marco in my thoughts but Alessia. And they weren't exactly thoughts, but fantasies.

I felt the goose bumps all over my arms, which strange because the water was warm and as I pictured

Alessia's long brown hair flowing over her shoulders, I realised I hadn't even seen her hair untied and that my weird mind was inventing images of the girl. I pressed two finger tips over my exposed outer lips and rubbed, gradually increasing the speed and pressure. Alessia's slender waist and broad thighs filled my mind as I slid my hands up towards her breasts and enveloped her nipple with my mouth.

I stooped forward and held onto the wall for support, using two fingers from my other hand to explore my, Alessia's depths. I trembled and my knee began to shake as, finally, an explosion of ecstasy erupted from the pit of my stomach.

I breathed and took a moment to gather my senses, blinking away the stars in my vision. Well, that was certainly a new experience for me, the first time in my entire life I'd masturbated to images of another girl - Just so long as she never found out, no harm done. Yes, it was a weird revelation, for sure, and I had to admit, it left me a slight bit confused.

Thankfully, a few minutes later, the answers came whilst occupied drying myself. I'd not been in contact with that many people lately and seeing another attractive person, even if a girl, had left myself with few alternative options for mental stimulation. Kind of like being in prison, in a way. I mean, what were the alternatives, Alberto? Had this occurred back home, hanging out with Alessia with men present as well, then I doubted I'd have been fantasising about her, but most likely one of the men. Of course, there was Marco but he had facial hair and I'd never been attracted to guys with facial hair and the man bun was hardly my thing either. The fact I'd chosen to masturbate to mental images of Alessia over Marco still felt weird but I had no doubt it was a one off. We'd only met yesterday and she'd made a big impression on me and now that was out of my system, I could persist with being a regular member of the heterosexual community, after my all too brief liaison, if only mental, with lesbianism.

A knock at the door jolted me from my thoughts and I threw on my dressing gown, tying the cord as I approached the door.

"Yes?" I asked, opening the door a few inches.

"Good morning, can I use your shower? The other one isn't working." It was Alessia who peered in through the small crack.

"Um, yeah, I guess so. I'm finished with it now anyway."

So I opened the door to let her in and she glided past, heading straight for my en suite without a second glance at me. She was wearing a fluffy plain white dressing gown, the smell of fabric softener flowing over my face as the floorboards creaked beneath her weight. I tried not to stare at her legs as she breezed through but it was either that or look straight at the boring brown door with not so much as a picture frame or streak of paint. And besides, she was only visible below the knees anyway; her slender calves exhibiting a touch of hard muscle each time she toed off the ground. The girl was in good shape, there was little doubt about that.

Now that I had company, it looked like I'd have to get dressed with Alessia showering in my bathroom, which under the circumstances felt a little weird for this virgin country girl. I really had to learn to get out a little more because girls did this sort of thing all the time and besides, there'd be a door separating us. Well, it wasn't exactly what I'd call a door but more a thin screen that folded open and closed concertina style.

Only, as Alessia walked through to the en suite, she neglected to close the screen.

Was the girl born in a barn?

Then all movement seemed to stop and no sounds came from within and I could only wonder what she was doing. She certainly hadn't yet stepped into the bath because I'd have heard and seen the shower curtain being pulled back. From where I was standing, the angle of the door frame prevented me from seeing what she was doing so I crept further towards the room's centre, my heart rate increasing, until gradually she came into view and I stopped. She was facing away from me whilst studying the shower control panel, fingers pinching her bottom lip. Suddenly her robe collapsed to the floor and her broad thighs and buttocks flashed before me as I twisted away with a silent gasp.

It all happened so fast that I hadn't been prepared for it and I dashed to the open shutters, closed my eyes and prayed I hadn't been seen gawping even as my memory conjured up images of Alessia's deeply tanned skin, the round shape of her bum and her toned thighs. Even as I opened my eyes, those shapes were still there.

What was happening to me?

The sound of plastic shower rings sliding across the iron railing struck me from my daze just as Alessia turned the water on and the steam began to swirl overhead.

Once again I found my head spinning and all because of this one pesky Italian. How would I survive the coming day?

Seriously, why was she taking a shower in my bedroom? Was this some sort of plan to get me interested? To get me thinking about her? Because it was kind of working, a bit, I think.

If I didn't find the answer, I'd explode. I had to know for sure. And I could do that by finding out whether the other shower truly was broken.

I dashed down the hallway and into the communal bathroom, closing the door after me. It was the one room on the top floor I'd not been in and why would I have, considering I had my own bathroom? Before Alessia's arrival, there were no other people who slept on this floor since Alberto and Maria were one floor down and I assumed would have use of their own en suite.

I gaped at the tap that would give me my answer, that would switch the shower on, or not, placed my hand upon it and slowly turned.

Nothing.

Alessia had told the truth.

She was not playing games.

I was probably turning insane.

Then, after a pause, there was a faint juddering that began to echo from somewhere behind the wall, the pipes probably, and then it increased in volume as the juddering morphed to a shaking. Fearing the awful noise would be audible throughout the entire house, I quickly turned the tap off, grit my teeth and perched on the edge of the bath.

Was I going crazy?

All this paranoia wasn't like me at all and I hated it.

Alessia had not lied and neither was she playing games.

It was all in *my* head.

And considering what her family were doing for me and how well I thought of her parents, I could only feel shame for my suspicions with regards to their daughter, their beautiful daughter Alessia. If there were any problems here then they lay with me, in my own mind and not her.

Enough!

No more, Dayna!

Get a grip!

I left the bathroom, feeling a renewed sense of clarity and as I did, Marco was leaving the room opposite. The same room which I knew belonged to Alessia. And what's more, he was wearing a robe. It was a light purple robe and far too small for him, which meant it could only belong to one person.

"Buongiorno." He croaked, yawning and wiping at his eyes.

So, Marco had spent the night with Alessia. I'd half suspected he'd be staying over anyway.

So why did it bother me so much?

THE FACT WAS that the entire city of Firenze was the true work of art. Actually going inside the Uffizi Gallery to gaze at Renaissance paintings and sculptures was a mere extension of that. The early September queues stretched around the sides of the five hundred-year-old inverted u-shaped building and being able to enter the gallery through a staff entrance was a giant perk.

The majesty of the main corridor was breathtaking. The floors were tiled with mosaics, the ceilings painted with intricate designs each as impressive as any of the canvases and all down the centre lay carved marble statues. One which demanded my particular attention was entitled Hercules and the Centaur Nessus. It resembled the Greek God Hercules clubbing to death what looked like a half horse, half man creature. When Marco saw my interest in the sculpture he launched into a well-rehearsed oration as to the story behind the work, stemming from Greek mythology.

As we progressed down the main hallway, there were numerous large exhibits in all the grand rooms. We saw masterpieces by Botticelli, Giotto, Lippi and Raphael.

Then we arrived in a large room which exhibited one of the most famous works of art in the entire world, a star attraction of the Uffizi.

Even though the museum was almost empty, there was already a large crowd gathered around Michelangelo's Doni Tondo. Marco told us how it was the only painting by the great artist in all of Firenze, which was still in its original frame. The painting depicted the Virgin Mary sat awkwardly, handing baby Jesus to Saint Joseph over her shoulder. Though what made this work of art so interesting was that whether Joseph was actually handing Jesus to Mary was still up for debate.

Marco didn't go into the intricacies of many of the paintings, just the ones we were more interested in and although I didn't consider myself an art expert, it was hard not to appreciate many of the masterpieces.

During the journey to Firenze, I'd promised myself I would chill out today and not allow my emotions to run away with me as they had earlier. Marco really was a blessing in that respect, since I could merely concentrate on the things he was saying, as well as the art in order to keep my mind off other things. Those other things were in the form of a tall, lithe and athletic girl named Alessia. She was wearing denim shorts, which I suspected she'd self-tailored from jeans and they showed off almost the entire length of her legs. She also wore a red sleeveless blouse, which not a great many girls would have got away looking so great in, yet not surprisingly Alessia looked incredible. I guessed it was the lush red against her skin, the perfect complement and then I remembered she was studying fashion in Milano and most probably knew of these small intricacies of dressing.

As we walked around the gallery, I tried my hardest to lead the way as much as possible. After all, if I couldn't see Alessia, particularly those legs that taunted me so much then the day would pass by all the more smoothly. From time to time there was no avoiding them and so I had to make a more concerted effort at marvelling the art instead.

Marco seemed to be struggling just as much as myself, to remain professional, even though he was used to Alessia, and at one point had to pull his eyes away when she was leaning over to study some pottery on the floor. Being a tour guide was just as much a relief for him as it was for me.

Where the gallery curved around for its second turn of the inverted u-shape, a small crowd gathered where a perfect view over the Arno River was visible. Marco stood behind me as we contemplated the vista.

It wasn't beautiful in a natural scenic sense. The best way of describing it was that some of the world's greatest architecture was sitting precariously over the raging water. The Ponte Vecchio or Old Bridge was the closest of several bridges that spanned the Arno. Whilst the bridges beyond were modern and uninteresting, the Ponte Vecchio was ancient and beyond miraculous. Shops and houses lined both sides of the bridge and from the side visible to us, it looked like much of the bridge was hanging over the water, only supported by beams jutting from the bridge itself.

To my surprise, it was not Marco, but Alessia who appeared to my side. "Do you see it?" She pressed her shoulder against mine as she pointed to the bridge.

"See what?" I scanned the entire length for anything obscure.

"The secret passageway." Her tone was filled with excitement, like she was giving away a secret that only she knew about.

"Secret passageway?" I half thought she was jesting. "No, I don't see it. Where is it?"

She leaned in so close that the smell of spices went straight to my brain and pointed to the north bank where old houses stretched up beyond the bridge. Then she tracked her finger over and along the bridge itself and then I saw it. I saw the secret passageway. She continued tracing her finger until her arm moved across the front of my body and then she was pointing to the south bank. Then she had to step forwards and point behind me as the secret passageway curved around and into the Uffizi Gallery itself.

"Oh, my God." I was awestruck. "But why?"

Marco smiled but let Alessia take it. "It stretches all the way from the palace on the north side, over the bridge, through the gallery and emerges in the cathedral. That's more than a kilometre."

I gazed again at the bridge and for the first time saw how, what at first I'd assumed to be the upper floor of the houses below, was, in fact, a passageway.

"The Medici family and the upper classes wanted to get to mass without having to walk through all the peasants below." Alessia laughed. "I used to dream it was my passageway to a secret beautiful garden." She said, smiling at me before laughing again. "Kids can be so silly."

"No, I don't think it's silly at all." I thought about the special place at the vineyard, where the stream trickled through the valley and how that was *my* secret beautiful garden. "I think it's sweet."

She beamed and once again seemed to have no comprehension of the concept for people's personal space, not that I minded but I was under control this time, thank God.

A few seconds went by in silence then Marco stepped closer. "The bridge has withstood wars, revolutions, floods, fires and even a mafia bomb ... A symbol of Firenze."

As we made our way out from the Uffizi Gallery, Marco told us about the German occupation of the city during the war. About how when the Nazis retreated north away from the pursuing allied forces, the many bridges spanning the Arno had been ordered destroyed. Yet on the Fuhrer's personal orders, the Ponte Vecchio was to be spared; a decision that would ultimately prove detrimental to the Axis powers, yet good for the city. Marco continued to elaborate about how people's individual experiences living under German occupation was not quite how the history books have made out. That many of the art pieces in the Uffizi were in fact kept safe by the Germans and many were lost only when the allies arrived in the city. "Hitler was, after all, an artist." He stated as a matter of fact. "There's a popular joke in Firenze, that the tourist occupation is far more oppressive than the Nazi one." He laughed and I wondered how many times he'd told that one.

I didn't think of myself as a tourist because I could happily live in Italy forever.

"But it keeps you in work." Alessia chided him and he threw up his hands in mock surrender.

"The stories this place could tell." I said to nobody in particular, realising that one day in the city was nowhere near enough time.

"Well, we should come back." Alessia said and I wondered if she'd read my thoughts.

I sighed, "I'd love to, Alessia, but there are so many other places I'd love to see in Tuscany and not enough time to see them."

She must have seen the regret in my face. "Well don't worry about all of that, we'll see them." She said, but I guessed she was just being friendly; she certainly didn't owe me anything. Besides, I had work to do at the vineyard. It was the reason I was here, after all, and I wanted to earn my keep.

We went for a snack in an espresso bar and Marco ordered over a plate of brioches, the pastry contrasting perfectly with the strong taste of espresso. There was nothing in the world as capable of kicking you into action quite like a real Italian espresso, the bitter taste remaining in my mouth until after we arrived at the Accademia, again jumping the queues as we entered.

The museum exhibited hundreds of canvases, sculptures and precious artefacts but there was only one real reason to come to the Accademia. The exhibits all led towards one great hall, which was the epicentre of the entire museum. The hall itself was long and narrow and opened into a dome at the far end. The narrow portion was dominated by four unfinished sculptures by Michelangelo. The sculptures were of slaves, still half encased in their original marble blocks, which gave them the aspect of being imprisoned within themselves, and had that been intentional then it was pure genius. Or maybe it was just destiny that they were never completed.

I turned away from the final slave and gaped in the direction of the dome.

And for a few seconds, I couldn't breathe.

Because there it was - Michelangelo's David.

From a distance, it dominated the entire dome and shrank everything and everyone around it. The many tourists that had gathered were not discussing it with their friends, taking pictures or else jostling for position but were instead stunned into a respectful silence, quite unlike anything else I'd ever experienced. It could have been like God himself had created something and placed it right here in this building for everyone to see and I couldn't wait to get closer.

I turned around to look for Marco and Alessia and after a few seconds saw them still standing by the first slave. Marco was waving a hand about the air whilst the other was lost somewhere in his ample hair. Alessia was staring down at the floor, only looking up to make the occasional word in a defensive posture. They both looked upset, Marco more so than Alessia and in the moment I felt bad for him. I'd experienced first-hand the kind of effect Alessia was capable of having on people and I was a heterosexual woman so I could only imagine how Marco felt if, as I suspected, he was in love with the girl. If that really was the case and Alessia didn't feel the same way then I couldn't imagine the anguish he must be going through. From what little I knew of Marco, he was a lovely guy and I wanted him to be happy. But I had to admit, even though it would feel a little weird for myself having to watch any romance between the two of them, it would come as a welcome relief knowing for sure that Alessia was interested in men. The knowledge that Alessia and Marco were a couple would serve to let me off the hook and I could go back to enjoying the rest of my stay in Italy, no complications.

"Where's Marco?" I asked Alessia ten minutes later when she found me below David.

She smiled but there was something behind the smile, like she was putting it on for me. "He'll meet us in an hour at Salvo's."

"Salvo's?"

"A friend of Marco's. He owns the restaurant where we're having dinner." She turned away from me to wipe at her eye.

I touched her on the shoulder. "Are you ok?"

"Yes, of course." She side stepped and began walking around the perimeter of the David. "It doesn't matter how often you come here, it always takes your breath away. Don't you agree?" She was squinting up at the beautiful statue, her words not matching her demeanour.

In fact, it was the first time I'd seen her looking vulnerable. Personally, I hadn't thought she was the type, yet here she was, and I wanted to hold her, to comfort her, even to allow her to cry whilst I held her in my arms but I knew that under the circumstances, that probably wasn't a good idea.

Out of a natural curiosity, I wanted to know what was said, what had happened, or what was still going on between them, but if I connected with this girl on a deeper level, I knew I'd end up getting too far sucked in, like had most likely happened to Marco. No, I needed to be extra careful with Alessia and maintain my policy of distance.

I moved close, but not too close and nodded. "The level of detail, particularly in the hands is incredible."

But who was I kidding? I could attempt to fool Alessia but I had to at least be truthful to myself. And the truth was that I lusted for this girl. But as long as it was just lust and nothing more than sheer lust then I'd be able to contain myself. I was the type of person who became attached to people far too easily, which was exactly why I had to keep my relationship with Alessia at a distance. Because if I ended up developing feelings for her on a deeper level...

...Well, it was too frightening to contemplate.

Thank God for art.

WE ENTERED PIAZZA DELLA SIGNORIA, the historic centre of Firenze. It had once been the centre of government for the nation of Florentia and now was home to a couple dozen Renaissance statues including a replica of David.

"It stands on the spot where the original spent much of its life." Alessia gestured to the David that guarded the entrance to the Palazzo Vecchio.

"You really are beginning to sound just like Marco."

"That's because I've been to Firenze with him too many times to count. Everything I know about this place is down to him." She no longer appeared upset, even at the mention of his name.

"He loves you doesn't he." I regretted asking as soon as the words left my mouth. I hadn't wanted to raise the subject at all but it was too late now and I cursed my stupidity.

She was quick to nod. "He tells me he's loved me for a long time. He's my best friend in the entire world and sometimes I hate what I put him through." She sighed and shrugged. "But I've made it clear to him, many times. I'll only ever see him as a friend."

What kind of friendship did these two share given that Marco had spent last night with her? And how many other nights? And thinking about it actually made me feel repulsed, to know how he felt, and that she still slept with him even though she never intended to commit. Alessia was exactly the same as so many other women I knew back home, the women who'd sleep with their 'boyfriends' even though they weren't in love. And I knew many girls who'd slept with guys they'd only just met, which to me really did feel wrong and I was so happy to be different in that regard. I wondered where Alessia fit within this demography?

"In fact, he was one of the reasons I wanted to get away, to go to Milano." Alessia confessed after a period of silence.

"Really?" If I sounded shocked, it's because I was.

"Oh my God, I can't believe I've just told you that." She blushed and turned to face the other side of the square.

I didn't know what to think. "Why did you want to get away from Marco? He's ok, isn't he?"

She turned swiftly back. "Oh, yes, of course, he's the best. Let's go to Piazza della Republica, it's a pretty walk." She was already leading the way.

She threaded her hand under the inside of my elbow so that now our bare arms were linked. Her flesh was soft and smooth but it was the sudden warmth of her skin I noticed the most, for it conflicted with the cool breeze that was uncharacteristic for a September afternoon in Tuscany. The warmth was physically comforting even if emotionally, I couldn't commit to the small gesture.

"It's just that I've known him all my life," Alessia continued, "and it's as though my entire life was pre-planned for me. Living in the countryside with few people my own age to grow up with. It was like I was expected to marry Marco and didn't have a choice in the matter."

"Oh, I see." I also grew up in the countryside but had never experienced having that one special friend like Marco. I could relate to her on some levels but not all.

"Nobody ever stopped to consider if *I* ever loved *him*, it was always just assumed, maybe because it was just so obvious and would make everybody else's lives easier."

"But you've told him? Why does he not move on and find somebody else?" I didn't think a guy like that would have much trouble finding an attractive Italian donna and I'd already noticed how other women looked at him. Heck, I'd more than noticed how other men looked at Alessia, which irritated me a great deal.

Alessia laughed. "I really wish it was that simple. I can't press a magic button and have him move on with his life." She stopped and turned to look at me. "I guess when you're in love with someone, it's not that simple to just move on."

However I felt, it was obvious Marco had it far worse. The poor man had suffered from unrequited love probably for years. I had no intention of falling into the same trap but there was something happening here, something inside me that I just couldn't control. The truth was, it was terrifying to my very core.

She linked back with me and we continued on our way, threading between crowds of tourists who gathered to see various street artists.

"And then there's the vineyard." She continued

with an added eye roll for good measure and I knew what she was about to explain. "Being an only child and therefore having the burden thrust upon me of being expected to go into the family business." She exhaled as though she was sick of the very subject. "For my parents, ideally I'd marry Marco and we'd work the rest of our lives on the vineyard. But nobody ever stops to consider me and..." she stopped as her voice choked, her face reddened and I worried she was on the verge of hyperventilation.

"Hey, it's ok. I understand now." For the first time, I emotionally accepted her warmth and to show it, I gave her arm a squeeze and to my amazement, not only did she squeeze me back, but she pulled me closer so that our hips crushed together as we approached Piazza della Republica.

And then it hit me. We'd connected. And in the moment I felt close to her. It was no longer just lust but the seeds of something else had sprouted in my heart.

And I was in deep shit.

"SORRY I'M LATE." Marco arrived at Salvo's with a stylish new leather man bag slung over one shoulder. "I'm not usually one for brand names but I couldn't resist this one." He took his seat, placing the bag carefully at his feet.

"Don't worry, we've only been here half an hour or so. Just time enough for one drink." I said, recalling how

Salvo had greeted us personally before giving us drinks on the house. "We met your friend, he's lovely."

"Yes, he is. It works out mutually beneficial too ... I bring tourist groups here for one of the best views of the city and my loved ones get seats like this." He opened his arms out to encompass the Duomo, of which the midsection and above were visible over the buildings that lay between the spectacular Duomo and Piazza della Republica, where Salvo's was located.

It was five in the evening and the first of the square's performers were unlimbering. There were four of them; three men and one lady.

"It's the Firenze Opera Quartet." Alessia declared. "They're one of my favourites."

"It's usually one of the same groups of people who perform." Marco said. "They have to pass an audition in front of the municipal council to be granted a license. On top of that, they're required to pay eighty euros for every spot they do. So they have to be good otherwise they lose money."

"That sounds a bit harsh. Eighty euros is a lot of money." I said, wondering how they managed to make a living as street performers.

"True. But Firenze is all about the tourism. We can't risk allowing some awful dead frog sounding singer scaring the Japanese away. We need their money." He laughed, I suppose he did have a point.

Salvo arrived and warmly greeted his friend. He was around Marco's age and had a similar sort of style to him; in fact, the two of them could have been brothers if it wasn't for Salvo's shaven head. I noticed the looks he gave Alessia, which bothered me, but thankfully Marco didn't seem to notice. Within a minute, free drinks arrived for everyone and it occurred to me that this was the second night in a row I'd be having drinks lavished upon me, which also meant it was the second night running that my uncontrollable emotions would be running away with me. It was always a consequence when I drank; I become attached to people, clingy and needy. Most often it was funny and people enjoyed being around me when I was in such jovial moods but here and now, it really wasn't what I needed.

"They don't serve Vino di Giordano here." Alessia observed to herself with more than a touch of irritation to her tone. "I'll be speaking to my mother about that."

I thought she'd wanted nothing to do with the family business.

Just like myself, Marco picked up on it immediately. "Alessia, why are you suddenly so interested in whether or not some small restaurant in Firenze offers your family's wine?" He was loud and uncaring of the other nearby patrons as he pushed his glass into the centre of the table, splashing drops over the side.

"I was just saying..." she said airily.

Marco shook his head. "You can't be half in and half out. It's not fair on your parents, your family's legacy and it's certainly not fair on me."

"I know, I know. Calm down, I didn't mean anything by it." She said in a soothing tone.

He leaned closer in and managed to stay subdued.

"Well, you can't keep doing this Alessia. You have to make your mind up one day." He pulled his wine back towards himself and almost gulped back the full glass in what was probably meant as a gesture of something. The drinks had only just begun, what would the rest of the night have in store?

"May I be excused a few moments?" Alessia stood and plodded in the direction of the bathroom.

After a short silence, Marco made a wild hand gesticulation and spoke. "I'd do anything for that girl, absolutely anything, but my God, is she ever stubborn. She could have it all, everything, but what she really needs is some sense knocking into her. She's about to throw it all away ... generations of her family's work and all because she's *confused*." He lingered on the final word, like he was repeating to me what Alessia had said many times to him. All he missed were the air quotes with his fingers.

I understood part of what Marco was saying, even some of the 'between the lines' stuff. But if Alessia was confused then that more than made two of us and I shuffled in my seat. "Look, Marco, I really don't think this is any of my business." Even though a large part of me wanted to know everything.

He nodded and his face softened. "I'm sorry, I'm not trying to involve you. Please, ignore what I said."

The food arrived and the three of us ate with the Duomo looming overhead. We each ordered spaghetti with differing garnishes; I ate a fresh rocket and tomato salad, Alessia a tuna and onion mix and Marco had some strange looking sauce that I couldn't decipher. As always, a large plate of crusty bread was placed in the table's centre and we each had a small side plate with a dollop of olive oil for dipping. Mercifully, the conversation stayed away from any of the growing list of loaded topics as Marco was happy enough talking about Firenze's past as well as the city's hopes for the future.

As we wiped our plates clean, a second bottle of chilled white wine arrived, which Marco opened and served out between us. He then sat back in his chair, hands clasped contently behind his head as Alessia and I talked amongst ourselves.

"What made you take fashion?" For a while now, I'd wanted to know about Alessia's life up north in Milano, as well as a few other things.

"I've always had an interest in colours and fabrics. There really is an endless amount of places you can visit in the fashion industry. A job at any half-baked Italian fashion house can enable you to travel the world." Considering she was talking about her chosen career, her voice lacked the passion she'd had earlier.

I wouldn't ordinarily have pictured such a girl, a tomboy sort, to have been interested in fashion, but then again, I also imagined that Alessia was full of surprises. "I guess being Italian offers you considerable advantages working in that industry?"

"You'd be correct," she shrugged, "an unfair advantage but I'll take it. Just like being a chef ... you say you're Italian and people automatically assume you're a good cook." She laughed. "The truth is I can't cook for shit, that's why I have my dad, or my flatmates in Milano."

Now it was my turn to laugh. "That is what confused me about you, Alessia, you really don't seem like the typical girly girl."

Her eyebrows lifted. "You're surprised I'd take fashion?"

"A little, yes."

She didn't answer her own question, which further reinforced in my mind it had something to do with escaping Tuscany, the vineyard and Marco.

My attention was drawn by Marco as he refilled his wine glass and he had a glassy look to the eyes and it was that, coupled with his silence, that gave me the impression he was in deep thought about something.

I picked up my glass and stared into the fluid. "So, what do you do for fun usually? I mean, up there in Milano?" I tipped the wine to my lips and swallowed a small quantity of the delicious liquid.

Alessia pulled her chair closer and I realised that at some point she'd managed to turn bodily toward me and away from Marco without my realising. One leg was crossed over the other as it made small bounces, her toes springing mere inches from my legs and I knew that if I dared look down, I'd have a bird's eye view of the inside of her thigh.

"Oh, just the usual stuff." She spoke slowly whilst continuing to bounce her leg. It was endearing, in a way. In many respects, Alessia was mature for her age, yet had many childlike qualities she obviously never grew out of.

"I meet with friends; we drink, we talk, we laugh." Her gaze scanned down my face and for a second I wondered if she was looking at my lips but then she shifted her attention to her wine, which she took without glancing at Marco.

Marco had meanwhile become a blur in my periphery and, hoping he didn't consider me rude for not involving him in the conversation, I turned to ask him the same question, when I felt a hand on my knee, bringing my attention sharply back to Alessia.

"And then there's my part time job." She said, her hand lingering and chilled from her wine glass. It caused no small chill that resonated up my spine, yet what I felt deep in my pussy was no chill, but something extremely hot. For a slow few seconds, I felt the paranoia that what was stirring down below, the emerging slippery discharge between my legs, would somehow reveal itself on my face. But then, mercifully, she removed her hand and I dared not look straight at her, but from the corner of my eye, I truly believed I saw the faintest curl emerge from the corner of her mouth.

I swallowed and kept my gaze fixed on the table, but wanting so badly to look at her. "Tell me about your part time job." And I didn't know if the reason I couldn't look was owing to my own fears, compounded by the moisture between my legs, that was even now running to my brain, or because Marco was sat so close and hearing everything.

"I work as a personal trainer in a gym. I really love

helping people achieve their dream look." Alessia said, almost as if nothing was amiss.

I thought of Patrick and how we'd met whilst he was working out in the gym. I'd always had a thing for fit men in tight tops; I was after all a hot blooded woman. Only now, it was images of Alessia in tight fitting lycra, lifting weights and stretching that flashed through my mind. Finally, things were beginning to make sense. It wasn't that Alessia looked like an athlete, even if she certainly was toned in all the right places and in that moment, I realised just what it was that had been driving me so insane about this girl.

"Well, that certainly explains why you look so fit." I said so feebly, whilst my eyes did most of the talking for me as they feasted on her almost non-existent waist before she broadened out impressively at the hips.

"I put a lot of hard work in but I'm pretty sure I get the desired results." She said with a smug expression, almost like she was tempting me to check out her body even more than I already couldn't help doing and it was more than tempting, even as her long slender leg continued pulsing off the other.

Even though I truly wanted to take in her specifics and fine details, to do so would be to further acknowledge my emerging interest in another woman. Not only that but there was still the matter of Marco. What was going through his mind right now? Did *he* think Alessia was flirting with me, or was it all in *my* head? After all, I had form recently, I'd been wrong about her and her intentions as short a time ago as this morning.

"Tell me about yourself." Alessia continued. "I can see you're also in pretty good shape." This time I was ready and waiting for any physical clue as to what was going through her mind and I could only watch as her eyes roamed down my chest, lingered on my hips and thighs, then returned slowly back, culminating when our eyes met.

There really was no doubting what I just witnessed and *felt*, as though her field of vision was like tiny hands pressing down on my skin - A complete thrill, I think.

There was a sudden loud guffaw from close by, Marco, and the loud scrape of wooden chair legs on tile shook me from Alessia's spell. "Of course! Everything makes perfect sense now." Marco stood, yanked the elastic from his hair in another physical gesture and leaned over the table, bearing down over the two of us.

"Marco? What makes perfect sense?" I asked, in some ways, hoping I already knew the answer.

He was standing straight now and began angrily ruffling through his hair as the neat little bun atop his head became unravelled. "I just can't believe I never saw it before. It was right in front of me the whole fucking time."

Alessia stood, tinges of fear flecking her face but it was mixed with something else, relief? "Marco, wait!"

He grabbed his bag from the floor, threw up his arm and stormed out.

Alessia made a quick apologetic glance at me and hurried after him.

"I KNOW WHERE HE'LL BE," Alessia told me as I emerged from Salvo's.

Marco must have run fast because when Alessia reached the outside, he was nowhere in sight. Thankfully she had waited for me because let's face it, without her I didn't know how I was getting back to the Villa di Giordano.

As it was, Marco was exactly where Alessia knew he'd be.

Walking across the Ponte Vecchio, you'd be forgiven for not realising you were on a bridge. Both sides were lined with jeweller's shops, all teaming with tourists, just as the bridge was itself, the old cobbles adding an extra element from a bygone era. At the midpoint, the bridge opened out where the shops gave way to a small plaza and now over a hundred people were gathered listening to a band playing in the open. Marco was perching against the wall, facing the singer and as we approached him, I couldn't help but feel devastated for him.

Alessia left my side and ran towards her friend, surprising him with an embrace from his blindside. I watched from a short distance away as Marco turned around and silently returned the hug, his face pressing hard against hers. Then he pulled away and placed his hands on her shoulders. I couldn't hear what he was saying but Alessia nodded and wiped away a tear.

"I hadn't meant you to find out like this ... I just couldn't continue..." I thought I heard from Alessia, which had only been possible due to a quiet beat in the music.

I decided to give them some privacy so I turned away to face the opening and the band in the bridge centre and I mused how directly above where I was now standing lay the secret passageway and I followed it along with my eyes as far as possible before it disappeared somewhere in the Uffizi Gallery.

"Dayna?" It was Marco who startled me.

"Hi, Marco, how are you?" I looked over his shoulder to where Alessia was standing, switching glances between us and the band.

"I wanted to apologise about before."

"No, you have nothing to apologise for."

"I shouldn't have made a scene like I did. But … as you know, Alessia, she…" He was calm and didn't show any obvious signs of distress, other than his now ruffled hair.

I flapped a hand. "Oh, don't worry about it. I'm beginning to see she has strange powers over people." I said in jest, though it was probably truer than I knew.

He ignored my joke and inhaled deeply. "In a way, I'm glad because I can now move on with my life. Just as importantly, so can Alessia. I want her to be happy."

"Do you think she has a girlfriend in Milano?" I asked, hoping Marco would know the answer.

He stared at me without a flicker of emotion. "Dayna, I think we both know there's only one girl she's interested in. So don't make this any more complicated than it needs to be. I'm done with complicated."

I shook my blurry head. There was one thing that confused me greatly. "But ... you spent the night with her?"

He laughed and looked up to the sky. "If only we *had* been doing what you obviously thought we were." He shook his head and the smile disappeared.

I was overwhelmed with a sense of relief. Alessia hadn't had sex with Marco whilst I was asleep in the next room. That revelation made me feel ashamed. Yet again, I'd jumped to conclusions about the girl. The fact was that Alessia was so much better than I ever gave her credit for, than I ever believed her to be. Perhaps she was so much better than what I deserved.

Considering all the confusion I'd experienced since meeting Alessia, that I now felt relief as well as a fluttering sensation in my belly, this release of tension resonated more than anything. Not only was I most certainly physically attracted to Alessia, that the thought of holding her against my flesh sent me insane, but I was also developing powerful feelings that I'd never felt for another person before, certainly no other woman. Could it really be love, considering I'd only known her a short time and that I'd been wrong about her on numerous occasions? All I knew was that all these feeling were new to me.

Marco sniggered. "If I could take a picture of your face. You look truly confused."

"It's my thinking face, I think."

Marco opened the leather bag that was strapped over his shoulder and pulled out a long jewellery box. "I was going to give her this tonight." He opened it up to reveal a beautiful silver necklace with a pretty pendant in an immaculate design. "It was kind of a last ditch attempt but I see now how stupid that idea was." He snapped the box shut with a thump. "In a way, I'd still like her to have it but under the circumstances, I doubt that'd be wise." For the first time in the conversation, he sounded on the verge of tears. "So I'm saving this for whoever does eventually come along, however long that'll take." He put the box back in his bag and secured the strap. "I'd also like to think I was strong enough to be able to stay around her, you know, continue as friends, like we've always been. I'm just not sure I have that kind of strength right now. I'm not sure if I'll ever see her again after tonight."

I felt so powerless, "Marco, I..."

He held up a palm to stop me mid-flow, not that I had anything significant to say that would help his aching heart.

"All I care about is her happiness, so please, just remember that."

"Marco, you will find somebody and you will be happy. You deserve it more than most." I rubbed his arm and I couldn't help but wonder if I felt him recoil ever so slightly.

He must have hated me, even though, as of yet, I hadn't really done anything. Marco seemed certain that Alessia and I were about to embark on a full blown lesbian relationship but the fact was that things were rarely that simple. Although a huge barrier had been smashed through, Alessia and I still didn't know each other that well.

All we had was a burning physical attraction and at least for my part, a deep curiosity.

Would that be enough?

It was twilight when Marco pulled the car onto the gravel that encircled the Villa di Giordano. I exited the vehicle, went round to the driver's side and shook his hand. I'd only known Marco a short time but I was still sorry to be saying goodbye.

Alessia remained in the passenger seat and so I left them in peace. Having known each other their entire lives, I didn't think the coming goodbyes would be easy for either of them.

The journey from the city back to the vineyard had been, for the most part, in silence save for the occasional beep of text messages from Alessia's phone.

The kitchen lights were on and from the outside, I could see Alberto doing paperwork with a glass of wine in front. I didn't feel like going straight inside so I set off down through the vines for a walk. The main pathway that meandered down the centre was lit with small lanterns hung from posts. Where the path ended and the stream began, the moonlight more than took up the slack from the lanterns.

The water made soothing sounds as it trickled gently by and so I sat down on the bank with my feet dangling over the edge. After a few minutes, I laid back on the grass and tried to make sense of the day's events.

I would need a long time to make sense of today, for I'd been taken completely off guard by Alessia and by my attraction for her. I'd started the day as a heterosexual woman, but now?

After around twenty minutes I was about to head back to the house but as I sat up I heard the faint tapping of footsteps from up the path. The sound grew in volume until a svelte silhouette emerged from between the lights.

My heart raced, the thumping in my chest growing harder and harder. I was upright, on my feet now and couldn't even remember standing. And then she was standing before me.

"I've come here for quiet moments my entire life." Alessia said, not quite invading my personal space as much as I would have liked.

"It's a special place. I like it down here." Time slowed down, my senses heightened, the water louder than before. I really didn't know what to say and should have had something prepared. Asking about how it went with Marco seemed the obvious and polite thing to do, but I didn't want to risk damaging this moment by mentioning him. What else could I say, other than... "How are you?"

She sighed and smiled. "Ok, considering ... but I think I need a hug."

"I think I can do that." And I stepped toward her, opened out my arms and wrapped them around her entire body, pulling her close. I felt her arms clasping around my back followed by a sudden exhalation as she squeezed tight. Her head nestled neatly in the crevice between the side of my face and shoulder. The smell of her hair, lush spices filled my existence. Her skin, so warm through her thin blouse. Our breasts pressed hard together. My knees trembled, I was afraid, so very afraid, yet couldn't let go.

I could feel her winding my hair into coils around her fingers and then she began to clasp large chunks of my flesh as I inhaled her smell.

God, I wanted her now, but this didn't feel right.

So I took a small step back and placed my hands on her shoulders. "We can't do this now, the timing isn't right. It wouldn't be fair."

"I know, I feel so bad right now." She sighed, the tears had stained her eyelids red and she gazed at my lips and I knew I wasn't strong enough.

She grabbed ahold of my forearms, which were still keeping us at arm's length, and then she was moving closer. My gaze switched between her big green eyes and sumptuous lips. I could smell her breath now, the faintest hint of sweet wine. We paused, our lips an inch apart as if to savour the moment a few beautiful seconds more. Were we really about to kiss?

And then our lips pressed together, softly, and I wrapped my arms tight around her shoulders. Her hands clasped hard around my ribcage as her tongue entered my mouth. Small sighs came from within her as I pulled harder against her back, our lips crushing harder together. My tongue connected with hers as they danced together in rhythm. Her hands slid up my chest, thumbs grazing my breasts before entangling in the hair behind my head. I ran a hand down her arm, across to her belly then slowly up to where I could grasp a heaving breast, the heavy and full globe filling my hand.

Suddenly, as our passion reached a sweet high, she pulled away with a hand against her lips.

"Alessia? What's wrong?" My heart was pounding so hard it might burst through my chest.

"Nothing, Dayna, nothing." Her eyes were fixed on mine as she smiled. "I just think it'd be better if we took things slow."

Of course, it made perfect sense. Jumping into sex immediately would not be the right thing for either of us, no matter how much I may have wanted it in the heat of the moment. There were still other considerations. I had a boyfriend, I was a guest at her father's house, I was only remaining in Italy a little under two months. How deep did I want to get into this when considering the small matter that I lived in a different country. Then there was the other small question of whether or not I was a lesbian – Not that the final point mattered much in the moment, yet conversely, it meant absolutely everything.

"Of course, we can take things slow," I reassured her, "I'd like nothing more than to get to know you better."

She held out her hand and I took it. We stood for a few minutes more, listening to the gentle drift of the stream. Then together we strolled back to the Villa di Giordano.

As we approached the door, we let go of each other's hand and returned to our separate rooms.

AT FIVE IN THE MORNING, I awoke to the sound of feet crunching on the gravel that surrounded the villa. I shot out of bed and dashed to the window, the first of the morning's light revealing Alessia as she threw a bag onto the back seat of her car before driving away.

CHAPTER FIVE

DISCOVERY

THE FIRST DAY WAS THE WORST.

Getting over the shock of her leaving like that. Not knowing why or for how long she'd be gone. If she'd ever come back. Was I to blame for it all?

"That's Alessia. That's my daughter." Alberto said, not bothering to look up from an ancient bottle corking device he was fixing after I'd asked him if he knew where she'd disappeared to. "What I wouldn't have given for a son." It was hard to tell whether he was joking. "Once you get beyond the falling out of tree stage, they're so much easier ... at least, so I've been told."

I ignored his dry humour. "Well, did she leave any indication of when she'd return?"

"No, she tends to float from one idea to the next. Women are like that. She'll come back when she feels like it." Clearly, he was well used to Alessia's errant ways and I wasn't sure how reassuring his words were. "Most likely she's back in Milano but who's to say? That girl has friends all over the country."

I thought about asking for her cell number but what was the point? She'd made the decision to leave and so chasing after her would be fruitless and I had no intention of making myself look possessive and deranged either.

We'd only shared a kiss, a wonderful, sweet and passionate kiss but nonetheless, it still felt like I'd been dumped. And it wasn't as if I'd been dumped by any old person, but by somebody who'd breezed in and out of my life and literally tipped it upside-down. And she was still having an effect on me, even now, without even being here.

A couple of days ago I was preparing to return to England and I'd be lying if I said the thought hadn't crossed my mind again. But important decisions made in times of emotional upheaval will rarely turn out to be the right decisions. My work experience here at the Giordano vineyard still remained an important part of my degree course and so I decided to grit my teeth and get on with the job.

The problem with monotonous jobs such as cutting grapes from branches all day is that you have all day to think. All you can do is think things through as your mind runs away during such tedious occupations. And so I was happy on the third day when Alberto offered to show me a different side of the wine making process.

"At this stage, we separate the white wine making process from the red wine making process." Alberto was turning a lever connected to a wheel that crushed the grapes in a giant oak cask. The juice flowed from a spout at the bottom and into another tub. "Because we're making white wine, all the skins must be separated. It's the skins that give the juice its red colour."

When the oak cask was empty, its contents taken from an entire cart that had taken me two hours to fill with harvested grapes, Alberto wheeled over the tub filled with juice and pumped the contents into a steel silo.

"From here, we add yeast and allow the juice to ferment for two weeks, which will turn the sugar from the grapes into alcohol. The carbon dioxide in the juice also disappears which will enable the wine to lose its fizz." Alberto said. "This part is the most time consuming of the entire process."

Considering the size of the winery and the dozen or so giant silos, once the grapes had been harvested, the rest of the process wasn't anywhere near as labour intensive. It just required lots of waiting for the wine to mature. Consequently, only Alberto and another employee, a local man from Poggibonsi named Francesco, worked in the winery. Francesco, grey haired and experienced, would often insist on showing me photos of his grandkids.

I watched Francesco discarding odd grapes he didn't approve of before scooping up giant bunches with a shovel and chucking them into the juicer. "We make premium wine here." He told me. "The overall grape quality is the primary factor in the finished quality of our product. One bad grape and..." he trailed off.

And so I was given the task of separating the bad from the good, filling the crusher and turning the wheel. It was bloody hard work and I spent hours turning that bloody thing and I knew I'd be sore the next day, only to begin the process again the day after.

There was much for my mind to take in and I was thankful for the mental respite. Brief moments where Alessia was not in my thoughts did happen by, but then she'd always pop right back in and a melancholy would fill my head until something else came along to distract me. And then the evenings would inevitably arrive and I'd find myself becoming depressed just as I had before Alessia had breezed in and out of my life. Only this time, it felt different. I was not unhappy through boredom as I was before. I was unhappy for a completely different reason and this reason was accompanied by a near constant feeling of nausea in my stomach. What's more, the Scalextric was broken and playing Ikari Warriors would only remind me of her.

A week after Alessia left, she still filled my every waking thought and it was during one of my many moments of boredom, my mind left to its own entertainment, that I discovered something for myself. You don't fall in love with a person when they're there with you. You fall in love when they're away and you're still thinking of them, always. Absence really did make the heart grow fonder, even if it was futile.

But time was ticking and I'd have to live with the very real possibility that I'd never see Alessia again.

It was after I'd finished crushing an entire batch of

grapes, my second of the day, and I was waiting for the last remnants of juice to trickle out into the tub when it happened. I grabbed the trolley lever and began to haul it toward the silos and I saw the still shadow extending far inside the building and the sun that framed the tall figure leaning against the doorway, staring inside at me.

I turned around to see who it was. "Oh my God." I couldn't believe it.

"Hello, gorgeous. I've missed you." Patrick said with that gorgeous smile grinning from ear to ear, his muscular figure filling out his white cotton shirt. He produced a single red rose from behind his back and I ran over to him, throwing my arms around his broad shoulders.

"Patrick? It's really you." I planted a giant kiss on his lips and felt the crush from his arms as he picked me up in a tight manly embrace.

"I missed you so much, babe." He said softly into my ear.

And in that moment, I realised, I'd missed him too.

"I ARRIVED last night and I'm staying in Poggibonsi, just a couple of days. I didn't want to turn up, surprise you and then find I couldn't stay in your villa." Patrick said as we strolled through the vines. "This place is stunning, you couldn't have asked for a better placement."

"Why did you think you wouldn't be allowed to stay?" I really didn't think there'd be any problem with it, Alberto was cool enough.

"Don't know ... perhaps your boss has the hots for you himself." Patrick chuckled and I punched him in the arm.

"Ouch! Your punches have gotten harder."

"That's what manual labour will do to a girl."

We were aimlessly heading in the direction of the stream at the end of the path and so I tugged on his hand and pulled him over to the left, heading instead for an orange tree and its welcoming shade. The sun was burning down and Patrick would be exposed to the heat.

We sat under the tree and I gathered up an orange that had fallen to the ground.

"Everyone says *hi*." Patrick said as he plucked up a blade of grass. "We all miss you and I for one can't wait to have you back home."

"I have about another six weeks here." I said matter of fact.

"I know, I've been counting but it's just going so slow." He planted another kiss on my lips, which I returned with a passionate embrace and he stroked my hair as our tongues connected. Then he pulled away, squinting. "Are you sure you're ok?"

"Yes, of course."

"It's just that..."

"It's just what?" I asked as I began to peel the orange.

"Nothing." His eyes lowered, distracted by the fruit.

I tore off a segment and handed it to him. Patrick was a good man, I respected him and enjoyed his company. But it just didn't feel right anymore, if indeed it ever had.

At seven in the evening, we met at a restaurant in Poggibonsi. Leonardo's was a traditional family restaurant decked out in an old world style, something I just couldn't escape from on this trip. I ordered a Margarita pizza, while Patrick had a sausage topping on his. Despite ordering spring water, I still found myself checking the menu for Vino di Giordano, which the restaurant did offer.

"When I got your email, I kind of panicked a bit." Patrick admitted and shook his head. "I didn't want you to throw your future away just because you were bored."

"You know how I can get." I said, not hiding the smile. He really did know me just as Marco had known Alessia.

"I came to give you a sort of peak during your many plateaus and hopefully make the rest of your stay a little more bearable..."

It wasn't as though it was unbearable, just boring, or at least it had been before it became extremely interesting. Now, it was just painful and I didn't think returning to England would nullify the pain.

"...And give you a little something to look forward to when you return." He said, though I didn't know what he meant by that.

"How so?"

"Dayna, you know how much I love you. And all this time apart has only reinforced my feelings for you." He reached across the table and took my hand. "Today would be seven months to the day since we started dating."

It took a moment for me to connect the dots, but he was correct. "You're right." How and why had that slipped me by? "Seven months, huh? You're such a plonker." I laughed but he didn't.

He waved it away. "Anyway, that doesn't matter, I'd still have come to see you regardless." His eyes transfixed on mine.

It hurt that I didn't feel the same about Patrick because I knew I'd have to break his heart. Soon I'd have to do the exact same to him as Alessia had done to Marco, the one difference being that we'd been in a relationship all this time and I still didn't love him – So why had I strung the whole thing out? Why had I mislead a good man and made him believe that there may have been a future for us when the truth is that I knew within weeks of meeting him that there wasn't. I'd wasted my time. But worse, I'd wasted the time of a person I cared for. It was time to let him go, just as Alessia had done for Marco. He'd hate me, but I'd be setting him free to get on with the rest of his life.

"Dayna, I think it's time we moved our relationship onto the next level."

"Patrick, I..."

"Dayna, I want you in my bed tonight!" He gave my hand a hard squeeze, so much so that it was hard to slip my hand out from his grasp.

"Patrick," there'd be no easy way of saying it, no matter what words left my mouth, "this isn't right. I just don't feel the same way." And I watched as the anguish built in his face.

There was a long pause as he tried to fathom my words. "Dayna, what are you saying?"

I took a deep breath. "This just isn't working out. I have to be honest with you, I don't think you're the right person for me."

His face momentarily screwed up and I could see he was struggling to maintain composure. "Dayna? Don't do this, please." He reached over and grabbed my hand again, his arm trembling. "Dayna, I've come all this way to see you, you can't do this to me, please."

"I'm so sorry. You deserve better. You deserve happiness. But it's not going to be with me." I squeezed his hand as hard as I could. I needed him to know I cared, because I truly did and that this was the single worst moment of my entire life.

He wiped tears from his eyes. "I thought there was something not quite right when we were under that orange tree before. I don't know what it is, but you've changed."

"That's probably the truth, Patrick. I realise how wrong it was for me to stay with you all this time, making you believe we had a future. But I was confused myself. Not that I'm making excuses." I don't know how I managed to keep composed myself but I knew I'd be crying tonight.

"Of course, you have to do what you think is best." He stood and placed some money down on the table. "I wish you all the best. But I want you to know, you're a bitch for wasting my time."

❧

THE BREAK UP with Patrick had served to provide another distraction from Alessia. That distraction lasted more than a week, even though the underlying misery caused by that girl still simmered below the surface. I was sure I wasn't suffering in the same way that Patrick was from the breakup since the greater part of my suffering was due to the girl and not Patrick. But I still felt really bad.

Patrick and I shared many mutual friends, friends who would now be out of bounds for me. Deep down I knew that one of the reasons I'd stayed with him was because I'd miss those friends if we broke up. Added to that, I guess it was just nice to be able to say that I had a boyfriend. I'd stayed with him for all the wrong reasons and endeavoured never to make the same mistake again, whilst a small part of me wondered if what had happened to me in Italy was some sort of karma.

I had only five weeks remaining at the Villa di Giordano and they would not be easy, though neither did I think returning home would solve my problems. It was two weeks ago when Alessia, that girl, had breezed into my world and transformed it. In less than two days she'd changed the entire course of my life, then left without a word. Two weeks after her leaving, I still found myself counting the days she hadn't been here. She was like a sickness in my heart, a sickness that couldn't be cured. The not knowing where she was, what she was doing and who she was doing it with was killing me and no matter how busy I kept myself, Alessia was always in my thoughts.

Every few days I would ask Alberto if he'd heard anything but the answer was always the same. He seemed amused by my constant questions about his daughter. "I had no idea you two had become such good friends." He'd said, apparently not realising that supposed good friends did not abandon each other like that.

But then, he didn't know the truth.

I finished crushing a batch of grapes before siphoning the liquid into one of the silos and when I went to collect the next cart load of harvested grapes, the cart bay was empty. "Honestly, I could run this place by myself." I said to nobody in particular. "Am I working too fast or is everyone else taking a break?"

I stomped outside, shielded the sun from my eyes, and stared down into the vines. Nothing amiss; people working but no carts. I sighed and treaded over the soft earth in the direction of where three carts were parked and sure enough, they were all full of harvested grapes, ready to be crushed. "Fine, I'll do it myself." The nearest person I could see was Mario but he was far out of earshot.

I took the brake off the wheel, absorbed the slow roll back down the uneven ground with my body and began pushing the cart uphill toward the winery. It was heavy and I realised it was the first time I'd attempted the task on my own, but slow and steady progress I made by using the power in my legs to heave the grape laden cart up the path, my cheek pressing against the side of one large crate for support. After a minute the lactic acid began to burn in my thighs and I almost began to regret that I'd bothered trying to do everybody's job on my own and hoped one of the guys would see me and run to help. Then suddenly it became easier as I hit the level ground so I took my face off the side of the crate and looked down. Only, it wasn't level ground and the slope was still steep. Then I saw the blurry figure in my peripheral vision and breathed.

"Thank you, Mario, better late than never." I grunted as a bead of sweat trickled off my forehead.

"Do I really look like Mario to you?" Returned the snappy feminine voice to my right.

My legs gave way and I'd have fallen underneath the cart wheels if it hadn't been for a desperate push against the cart with my arms that sent me tumbling sidewards into the earth. I landed on my back between two vines.

Alessia stepped away in the opposite direction, in hysterics, just as the cart began its fast descent downhill.

I scrambled to my feet in time to see Mario leap out from the path of the wayward cart.

"Serves him right for not helping." She managed to say through laughter.

I gaped at her as I shook earth, leaves and God only knew what else off my clothes and out of my hair. "You're back!"

"I'm back!"

~

"You DIDN'T HAVE to sneak up on me like that." I turned my back on her and began stomping back down the path.

Mario was straining as he swung the cart out of a patch of dirt and back onto the track. It really was a miracle the thing hadn't tipped over, crushing several hours work in the process.

The patter of Alessia's footsteps followed close behind. "Well, you're happy to see me aren't you." She said with sarcasm.

"No, you should have stayed in Milano." I said over my shoulder.

"I wasn't just in Milano."

"I really don't care." I pointed at Mario then nodded to the cart. "You wouldn't mind helping out this time, would you?" The words sounded curter than intended.

"Si, signora." Mario positioned himself and waited for me.

"It's ok Mario, I'll do this." Alessia said as she stood to the side of the man.

"No, we don't need you. Look what happened last time. I could have been hurt." Those words also sounded curt, but not as curt as I'd have liked. "Ready Mario." I thrust my shoulder into the cart as Mario did the same.

I lost sight of Alessia during the push back uphill because the cart was blocking my view but as we hit level ground I did catch a glimpse of her back just as she entered the villa.

"See if I give a shit, Mario." I told him in English as we approached the winery but he gave no response.

I crushed that batch in record time, heaving on that

wheel and pounding the grapes into mush, pretending Alessia was in there too and laughing as I did. Then I wheeled the fruits of my labours toward the silos and saw the other two filled carts that had already been manoeuvred into the bay. At least I wouldn't have to do it myself this time.

I dipped the hose into the juice barrel and turned the lever attached to the wheel, which sucked the liquid into the silo. I was finding a good rhythm when two hands grabbed my arm and pulled me away.

"This way." Alessia said and then we were striding towards a door which she opened, pushing me through and then closing and locking it behind us.

"Just what is the big idea?" I threw her hand off my arm.

I knew the room to be some sort of storage area, although I'd never been in it before. Though now I was here, it resembled more a cupboard than an actual room and its small confines gave me a slight claustrophobic feeling. Disinfectant and other cleaning materials were stacked on shelves along with what looked like spare parts for the various machines in operation, not that I paid much attention to those details in the moment.

"I know you're angry and you have every right to be." She was forced to stand so close that I couldn't even see what she was wearing on her legs without tilting my head down. As it turned out, they were bare, as usual, a fact that didn't help when I was trying to be angry with her. She was probably wearing the exact same self-tailored denim shorts she'd worn in Firenze, which had played such an important role in winning me over. She was also wearing a green sleeveless stretchy top, which her breasts were trying their damnedest to push through. I wondered if she'd been wearing sports bras on all the other occasions I'd seen her because they'd never appeared so large before. I knew for a fact she'd been wearing one under her running top when we'd first met. But back to the moment - Because I could swear she'd been inside and changed into something she knew I wouldn't be able to resist.

And how could I resist this Goddess as she stood so close that I could feel the warmth from her body, her breasts almost touching mine due to the strict confines of the room. But I didn't want to get hurt again, so resist her I would have to do, no matter how hard it might be.

"Angry? Who's angry?" I looked her deadpan in the eyes, as serious as I could. God, but all I wanted to do was rip her clothes off but she'd treated me as if I didn't matter and I was not about to be best friends with her just because she decided to breeze back into town. For all I knew she'd be gone again this time tomorrow.

"You're obviously very angry." She touched my arm and I batted her away. "See! I knew it. How can you say you're not angry when you're clearly very angry?"

Her face was full of smug mischief as clearly, she was enjoying this, testing and teasing me, daring me to laugh and laugh I easily could, if only I wasn't so angry. Still, it took a big effort to stop myself from falling into hysterics, and it was an even bigger effort to save from making up with her right there right then and in a way I'd remember for the rest of my life.

The whole situation was ridiculous. Here I was, having been bundled into a store cupboard, stood toe to toe with this beautiful girl who I hadn't been able to stop thinking about since the moment I met her. And now she was all but demanding that we resumed where things left off. How had my life come to this? She sure caused problems when she was away. But when she was around she was like a tornado that messed up, destroyed and rearranged everything on my inside.

"No, Alessia, you'd have to matter for me to be angry." I prayed that my face did not give away what I felt in my heart, even though on many levels, I guessed and even hoped she knew exactly how I felt, what I wanted to do to her.

"I don't matter to you?" She asked in a doubtful tone.

I exhaled long and loud, making a show of it. "No Alessia, you don't matter to me." Except I was making no attempt to leave and her smell was already doing strange things to my brain.

"I'm back home forever. I just wanted you to know that." She was looking hard at me, doubtless trying to gage my reaction to her news and I wasn't sure how great my poker face was.

"Really?" I chirped and immediately regretted my need for clarification.

Her lips curled up ever so slightly and her feet scuffed on the floor as she moved even closer. "Yes. Take a look in my car. I've brought all my things back from Milano."

I sighed and moved my head away. "Whether you stay or leave, it matters little to me." Even as I spoke, my heart was filling with joy and hope. I may only be around for another five weeks but if Alessia would be here throughout that time, it would be far from boring. The thing was that I couldn't say whether that would be good or bad.

She leaned back, propping her elbow on a shelf and as she did her breasts pushed out that little bit further. She was almost certainly testing me and I bet she was enjoying it too. "So you're not in the least bit happy I came back then?" The sheer audacity of the girl and I'd be lying if I said I didn't find her exhilarating.

I stepped forward, closing the gap she'd created a few seconds before. She was taken aback by the sudden rash move and in the moment, I just lost control of any restraint and if I'd wanted to play this as though I didn't care, then she had me beaten. "Alessia, you arrived in my life and changed it all in a single day. And then against my better judgement, I gave into you when I knew you would hurt me. You left without saying a word to me, without a single word of where you were going or for how long. You must be some arrogant piece of work if you think you can simply turn up again and I'll come running to you." I watched as her mouth dropped open, finally looking a little sorry for the pain she'd put me through the last couple of weeks. "Would you please stay away from me!"

I turned around, unlocked the door and yanked it open before stomping straight for the villa.

As I passed Alessia's car, I noticed how it was packed with her things.

I FIGURED it was about time I finished work and so I headed straight for my room after what could only be described as an experience with Alessia.

Sure, I was still angry with her, but in no way did I truly wish for her to *stay away from me*. In fact, a large part of me wished we'd have kissed and made friends in that little room; it sure would have been interesting. But if I made it too easy for her to win me around then she'd only end up taking me for granted in the future. No, I had to make her work for me, at least a little bit. Since her return, I'd knocked her back twice, something I had a feeling she wasn't used to experiencing.

Besides, she still hadn't told me why she'd left and what she was doing whilst away. It felt good to be the one in control for a change.

I heard a car door slam and so I went to the window and looked outside. Alessia was going to and fro between her car and the villa, bringing in bags of luggage and various obscure shaped objects. I had a great view of her straining from the effort as I sat on the window ledge, pretending to read a book. A couple of times I caught her glancing up at me and I was half tempted to wave but thought better of it. When the last of her belongings were taken from the car, she locked the doors and entered the house for the final time. From then on I had the pleasure of listening to her trotting up and down the steps, from the bottom to the top floor, groaning and complaining from the labour as she carried her things to her bedroom.

Throughout, I was reading The Prince, by Nicolo Machiavelli, a classic piece of Italian literature, though I was having too much fun to fully concentrate as I giggled to myself. On more than one occasion, Alessia's panting was loud enough for me to hear through the closed bedroom door and twice she kicked at a step in rage. I knew it was mean of me to be revelling in the girl's misfortune, but perhaps if she hadn't abandoned me then I'd have been more than willing to help her out.

From the window ledge, I saw Alberto leave the house, climb into his van and drive away down the path and out through the gates. There was nothing unusual in that, since Alberto regularly left the house at this time for extended periods. However, what it did mean was that for the first time ever, I was alone with Alessia.

My belly rumbled. It was time for an aperitif and so I put down the book and left the room.

Alessia was coming up the final step with a large box in her arms so I stepped aside, allowing her to pass. The faint smell of body odour mixed with spices brought back the memory of the time we met after she'd been jogging. She glanced at me, sweat pricking at her forehead and so I gave her a smile and continued down the stairs, noticing the huge pile still stacked by the door. Oh, the poor girl.

I opened the fridge and put together a tasty aperitif of

thin bread slices with cheese, parma ham and sundried tomatoes. I poured a glass of Vino di Giordano and carried the meal back upstairs. I didn't pass Alessia on the return trip, but I did see her, through her open bedroom door, tipping a box full of what looked like running and other training gear onto her bed. From the look of her room, she wasn't a tidy person and I wondered to what extent that reflected her mind.

I perched myself back on my window ledge, ate the aperitif and sipped wine whilst attempting to read Machiavelli.

Twenty minutes later there was a knock at my door.

"Yes?" I asked, still at my perched position.

The door creaked open and then Alessia's head peeked through the crack. "May I come in?"

I hesitated for a second and put my wine down on the table. "You may."

She crept inside and closed the door after her. Immediately, I was aware that whatever game I'd been playing the last hour, however much I felt like it was me who was in control, one look at her in those jogging bottoms and that sleeveless top as she entered turned my legs to jelly, my mind to mush. No, it was Alessia who was in control, not I and for the first time ever, we were now truly alone, all by ourselves and my jelly legs trembled from what I could only describe as anxiety, bordering on true fear.

She half closed the gap between the door and myself so that now she was standing only a couple of metres away. She'd changed again since our little rendezvous in the store cupboard, perhaps due to her prior exertion from all the lifting and carrying but I'd never seen her looking so beautiful, her ponytail draped over one shoulder and down over her front as she clung to it with both hands. I'd never seen her looking so vulnerable either and I wondered if she was as petrified as I was.

"Hi, Dayna. I just wanted to say that I'm truly sorry for leaving like I did. It was wrong of me, considering everything." She didn't look at me as she spoke, but to the floor, with only the occasional glance upward to meet my eye. "It's just that, as you know, I wasn't right with my head, with Marco and everything. I just needed some time away to come to terms with losing my best friend and..." she paused and looked up to meet my eyes.

"And what, Alessia?" I asked, praying she was about to say what I hoped.

She took a step closer and I hated that she could never invade my personal space when it mattered the most? I wanted her flush against my body.

"With losing my best friend and..." strands of her hair came loose from the constant twisting and pulling, "...and my attraction to you."

I stood and closed the gap some more so that if I reached out I could touch her. My legs held, I don't know how but they did.

"I've wanted you since the moment I first saw you." Her tanned skin blushed red. "When I was away, you were all I thought about. It nearly made me sick. So now I'm back and I'm not going anywhere."

For a few brief seconds, my eyes glazed over, unaware

I was crying. "Oh, Alessia, you have no idea how good that is to hear." I spluttered.

She let go of her hair and closed the small space between us raising her hand to wipe away my tears with her thumb. The beautiful gesture caused me to laugh, a world of heartache leaving with it. Then she gently brushed her thumb across the entire length of my lower lip so that I could taste the salt from my tears.

I reached up and grabbed her forearm and then we both stopped in recognition of what we were doing, only looking at one another, barely daring to breathe for fear of spoiling the moment. We were close now, so close that spices filled my head, the pupils of her green eyes enlarged and her chest heaved in unison with mine, our breasts just barely grazing together.

I let go of her forearm and as I did, she lost her hands in my blonde locks, grabbing swathes and threading them through her fingers, pulling my face just that little bit closer to hers so that I could feel her warm breath on my skin. I clasped my free hands around her slim waist, squeezing and feeling her lithe physique below the thin material of her top. I'd always thought she possessed the most impressive hourglass figure and I marvelled at how my hands moved apart as I ran them down her hips. I pulled her into me so that our thighs crushed together and then our lips were inches apart. She switched her gaze between my eyes and lips and I knew I was unconsciously doing the same.

"I've never wanted anything so much." I groaned as I brought my hands up to hold her face. It was no longer just lust for me but so much more than that and I surrendered to the thought of giving myself to Alessia.

Her smell, her sweet natural smell overwhelmed my world as our lips neared and she closed her eyes in preparation as I did the same. Finally, our lips pressed softly together, sending a bolt of energy down my spine to resound in my toes. Her tongue found its way into my mouth as it slid along the inside of my lip. My tongue connected with hers as I reached around and pulled out her hair bobble. I arched back and watched as her long brown hair unfurled before my eyes, sending a wave of spices washing over me.

With a devilish grin, she fanned out her mane. "You know, very few people get to see me with my hair down." If that was true then she was denying the world something special. Her hair begged for my touch, so I ran my hands through it, the silky texture flowing through my fingers, the smell of yet more spices flooding my existence.

I stepped toward the bed, pulling her with me and that was when I felt the wetness between my legs. Oh God but this was truly about to happen. Though there was just one thing left on my mind, just one confession I needed to make, that I needed her to know. "Alessia, this will be my first time." I knew my pale skin was turning red from my embarrassing admission.

She sighed and smiled, pausing for a few seconds before speaking. "And you will be my first."

"No, I meant, you will be my first time with anybody. Not just with a woman." I suddenly felt more vulnerable than ever and was about to retreat into myself when she reassured me.

She laughed, tilting her head to the ceiling, then slowly looked back to me. "And I meant the same."

She laughed, I laughed; a mixture of relief, happiness and emotions I just couldn't describe. It was all so perfect. But it was about to get so much better.

"Take your top off." She demanded, grabbing my blouse from the bottom and forcing it over my head, apparently unable to wait for me to remove the barrier myself. "You have no idea how long I've been wanting to see you in your bra." She threw my top to the floor and brought her hands up to cup my breasts, moving her gaze between the two large globes as she caressed them and my eyes to gage my reaction.

But my bra was still on, after all, it wasn't like either of us were practiced at this, so I reached around to unhook it and she gently slipped it off before returning her hands to my breasts.

My body trembled. It was an intense moment having this girl's hands on my body like this. But I was not about to wait another second before I got to experience Alessia's breasts heaving in my hands. Her sports top was tight against her skin, an incredible turn on for me, but it would have to be removed nonetheless. I pulled it up, the material stretching as I did, and then it was over her head, her arms raised, ever so slightly flattening her breasts. And then she watched for my reaction as she lowered her arms and her breasts settled into place, though in reality, they were so firm they barely moved in her sports bra, which took me all of three seconds to unhook and throw to the floor.

I exhaled without realising. Two large, perfectly pert breasts demanded my attention. Her nipples were small yet stood hard and stimulated. I couldn't wait another second and I brought my hungry hands over them, pressing, feeling their weight in my grasp as they more than filled my hands. I wanted my mouth over her nipple, to flick my tongue over and across it, but I could wait, though not for long.

Alessia grinned with pride, gaging my reaction to experiencing her body that she'd put so much effort into sculpting. She knew she was hot and that made her all the sexier. "I can see you like those." She said with total conviction, obviously revelling in my perversion.

It was an understatement. "You're the most perfect thing I've ever seen."

She pulled me into her with an unexpected force and our breasts crushed together; blonde against brunette. We kissed for several minutes and then I felt her hand on the front of my skirt as she fiddled with the buttons before it came loose and fell to the floor.

I stepped out from it and gestured to her jogging bottoms. "Hey, I'm going to need you out of those things too you know."

She didn't hesitate and removed them in a matter of seconds to reveal her long, tanned legs. They were slender yet sculpted, her muscle tone barely visible to the eye, but more than evident to the touch, as I found out when I caressed my hands down their entire length.

"I never took you for such a pervert, Dayna." She joked, but I just couldn't help it. The truth was, I never knew myself to be a pervert before this very moment.

I ran my hands back up the length of one long thigh, slowly standing as I did and found my hands grasping at her underwear, some black sporty things and I gently grazed her pussy through the fabric. She bucked from the sensation and saw my wide grin as I felt how wet she was.

"You really want this don't you." I already knew the answer and loved teasing her, she deserved it.

"You have no idea how badly I want you." She fixed her gaze on me and everything stopped as I felt her hand on top of mine. "This is it, Dayna. I want you to have me. There's no going back now."

I nodded. "No going back and I wouldn't stop for the world."

She removed her hand and then I slipped my thumbs inside her underwear, feeling the tension of the tight elastic. I crouched down and slowly tugged her underwear down her legs, always keeping my eyes on them as they moved towards the floor. She stepped one foot out then used the other to lift them towards my hands. I grabbed the damp garment, brought it to my nose and inhaled its heavenly scent before gathering my composure and throwing it atop my luggage, a souvenir for always. My eyes were level with her pussy, but I'd been delaying that pinnacle moment of actually gazing at my prize. I felt her hands running through my hair as I slowly tilted my head up and then I saw it.

The mere sight of her petite pussy, glistening with

moisture sent another wave of exhilaration shooting through my body. She was shaved and I wondered if she'd anticipated having sex with me this night; such was Alessia's confidence, it wouldn't surprise me one bit.

I stood and gently rubbed my fingers over her outer lips, revelling in feeling her shudder from my touch. But I'd got carried away here, which couldn't be helped.

"Hey, I have to remove yours." She sighed, almost like she could read my mind and without waiting, hooked her thumbs inside the fabric of my white knickers to slowly pull them down the length of my legs, caressing and kissing my flesh as she moved. I lifted my feet as she slipped them off and watched her smile as she felt the moist fabric with her fingers. "I'll be keeping these too." She shot me a devilish grin and pressed them against her face, inhaling my essence.

Then she stood, we shared a look and embraced each other, acknowledging our now entirely naked bodies and vulnerability, experiencing this event together. We kissed some more as our hands explored each other's body; mine devouring her hard buttocks as she seemed obsessed with my breasts. Then she clasped my bum and together we pulled our hips hard against each other, rubbing our pussies together, mixing our juices.

"What are you going to do to me, Dayna?" She whispered sweetly into my ear, taking a hold of my hand.

I was never usually one for dirty talk, but I knew full well what I wanted to do to her so I whispered back, "I'm going to kiss every inch of your body and then make you cum like never before." I could hardly believe my own mouth capable of producing such filth but there was no word of a lie in it.

With my hand in hers, she backed up towards the bed and laid on her back, gently pulling me down with her. I positioned myself over her body and we kissed passionately for several minutes before I moved onto her neck, an area where I loved being kissed and I was happy to see the effect I was having on her as she trembled beneath me. Her skin was so soft and clear, the smell divine as my nose nestled between her neck and hair.

I worked my way down to her collar bone and enjoyed her reaction to my kisses in that sensitive area. Then I ran my tongue down her body, tasting her skin until my eyes were level with her breasts. They were flattened slightly due to her laying down and finally, I would have my way with them. I seized one large breast in my left hand as I stroked her hair with my right. I gazed longingly at her nipple, stiff and pointed and drew my tongue over it once, she jerking from the sudden warmth and then I enclosed my mouth over it, sucking, nibbling and pressing my tongue against it, tasting her. Alessia's beating heart resounded in my ear and she hummed from somewhere deep within. A large tremble came from her midsection as I felt her hands losing themselves in my hair.

But I now wanted, no needed, to venture further, to experience the most intimate part of this girl and nothing would stop me. As I released her nipple from my mouth and began meandering kisses down her abdomen, as she trembled, I knew she was filled with trepidation and nerves, yet also with energy and fire.

I reached her belly button and she laughed as I wiggled my tongue in and out, making a mental note for later about how ticklish she was there.

I continued my slow journey down, her breathing increasing in intensity and I sensed her hands reaching for the bedposts. She would need something to hold on to, considering what I planned on doing to her.

My lower body ran out of bed space and so I stepped onto the floor to gain a better angle and then my eyes were level with her pussy; her beautiful, glowing, wet pussy. It was ready for me and I wouldn't delay any longer.

I glanced over her hips, wanting to look one last time into her eyes before I went down. She raised her head from the pillow and caught my eye. Want, lust, fire – They were all there, with the slightest hint of fear. She reached forwards with one hand and I grabbed it as our eyes fixed on each other's, acknowledging this new territory – Everything would be ok, we were doing this together.

Then her head dropped back and as I ran my tongue once along her outer walls, scooping up her nectar, she shuddered and squeezed my hand tight. Her lower back arched from the bed, then settled and again, my tongue glided up her slick lips. She squeezed my hand again then released it as her hand shot back towards the bedpost.

I continued, working my tongue around her clit before moving onto her bud. She bucked hard and then I held my mouth over it; licking, sucking, nibbling, experiencing, all whilst my fingers lovingly stroked her inner thighs.

She panted hard, loud and in a rhythm I matched with my tongue, her taste finer than any of Italy's wines and I wanted more.

I brought my hand inside and positioned a finger at her entrance. She was absolutely dripping and more than ready and so I continued rubbing her pussy in circles, feeling her whole body jerk from my touch, again and again, before finally, I slipped my finger inside her depths, feeling her moist, wet walls. Whilst maintaining a steady rhythm with my tongue, my finger also delved away, searching slow and gently, in and out. I pulled my finger out but only so I could enter again with two and as I did, she groaned from somewhere deep inside.

I curled my fingers and rubbed with increasing pressure against her inner walls, matching the rhythm with my tongue, which also matched the flow of her breathing. Her breaths increased in speed, in volume, in profundity and I knew she was close to exploding.

I maintained the rhythm, felt her pussy clenching tightly around my fingers as her bud swelled in my mouth and she began swearing in Italian, words I didn't recognise.

Her back arched off the bed to such a degree I had to alter my position. Her body went into throes, between jelly and rigid. Finally, she screamed, her knees shook and her entire body seemed to flush cold as her juices gushed out from within her opening to dribble down my wrist. I pulled out and, using my tongue, scooped up the nectar from my hand before returning to clean up every last drop from her opening.

She was still undergoing the last few seconds of nirvana and I wanted to experience it with her so I moved up to her on the bed and was rewarded when she threw her arms around me, almost driving out the air from my lungs, a possessed look in her eyes. She held me tight, our naked bodies pressed hard together, the heavy perspiration from her flesh cool as she shivered in my arms.

"Dayna…" she groaned and kissed me hard on the lips, "I have never, ever…" she exhaled loud and long.

I was worn out and Alessia looked spent as well but then she surprised me by reaching down to stroke my pussy. I shook as we held each other and she made soothing tones in my ear and I just wanted to melt into her.

"You are so wet." She whispered, her breath so hot in my ear. And then I felt her enter me but only slightly. My body jerked and she kissed the side of my face, massaging my clit with her palm as her fingers delved that little bit deeper, her free hand pulling on my back so that our breasts were always flush together. I wanted to scream but instead stifled it by pressing my lips to hers, our tongues connecting but barely moving. I groaned, it came from deep down in the pit of my stomach.

But she couldn't get any more purchase at that angle, so she released her grip and leapt down to my hips. I briefly saw her crouched on all fours from behind before she turned round, a perfect image I'd keep in my mind forever.

Then, losing all control over my body, my hips lifted from the bed as I felt her tongue sliding over my lips, the sudden heat startling me. Her mouth enveloped my clit and my body tensed up. I looked down; my nipples were solid, her head buried in my most intimate area.

My breathing grew deeper and louder and I felt her tongue twisting inside my passage, devouring the juices my body continued to create as a reaction to her. The taste of salt grew heavy on my lips, the hairs on the back of my neck standing on end. I felt her fingers enter me, pressing, rubbing up and down the inside walls. I bucked again as her mouth enclosed hard around my engorged bud, her tongue flicking against it, sucking and biting.

I pulled so hard on the bedpost, I worried I'd remove it from its fixture. My body quivered, my breathing deep, her tongue, her fingers matching my beat.

I screamed. "Alessia! I'm coming!" My body exploded in a frenzy, my hips raised from the bed, my back arched to an obscene angle, my juices streamed from my opening and I felt her tongue dashing to collect its prize. Only when she'd devoured every last drop did she leap back atop of me. I clung to her. We remained locked in an embrace for what seemed like forever and I never wanted to let go.

Only when we regained composure did we kiss, slowly and with a deep passion I'd never felt before.

"Alessia, what did you just do to me?" Came my hoarse voice.

She panted her response. "That was quite an experience."

I gazed at Alessia, her beautiful face and knew I never wanted anybody else. "Alessia, I think we have things to discuss."

She smiled and I immediately knew she wanted the exact same thing as myself. "We definitely do."

We remained held close, trembling for a while until finally climbing under the covers and it took us all of thirty seconds to fall asleep in each other's arms.

EPILOGUE

Luckily, Alberto slept on the floor below and never came upstairs where Alessia and I had our bedrooms.

Every night, Alessia came and stayed with me, apart from those nights where I slept in her room. The sex became better and better, which after the first night, I really didn't think was possible.

As my time in Chianti drew to an end, I began to worry about what to do. I was madly in love with Alessia and hated the thought of being parted from her, even for a short amount of time. It was a subject we'd have to discuss and soon.

Alessia told her dad about dropping out of university and with mixed feelings on the subject, he gave her a job on the vineyard. She took care of the accounting as well as running the newly opened wine shop, which proved extremely popular with tourists visiting for wine tours.

She kept busy and loved her new job, which of course pleased Alberto.

It was when I had only two days remaining when we received a surprise guest at the vineyard. Marco stopped by with the news of his new love, a stunning Swiss brunette he'd met during one of his tours. She'd been taken in by his charm and enthusiasm and he'd asked her to meet with him for dinner whilst on the Ponte Vecchio. Within days they were in a relationship and she endeavoured to move to Italy to be with him.

Marco had something else, a present for Alessia and me.

"You can't buy these and if you only knew the strings I had to pull to get them." He handed over the tickets for the secret passageway in Firenze. "But I knew you'd love them."

The next day, Alessia and I arrived at the cathedral in the city centre and were ushered into a private room where the secret entrance was hidden behind a regular looking door that aristocracy had walked through for hundreds of years. We walked hand in hand through the passageway beginning in the cathedral, to emerge in a beautifully ordained corridor in the Uffizi Gallery surrounded by artwork that the general public never got to see. Following a few turns, we were then walking alongside the Arno River until a covered bridge took us over the road and then we were walking above the shops on the Ponte Vecchio, staring out at the tourists on one side and the river on the other. The ceiling was covered in immaculate designs and I thought it a pity that all this magic was closed off to the people. After the bridge, the passageway became lost in a tangle of houses, shops and buildings. Then the passageway, supported on several pillars and archways, entered the Pitti Palace before opening up into another resplendent room. Suits of armour from the Medici period stood imposing against the walls.

"I've wanted to do that my entire life." Alessia said as we left the palace at the back and found our way into the Boboli Gardens, an ancient garden built by the Medici's.

"It really is a passageway into a secret garden." I said to her as we emerged alone into a grand opening with a lake and fountains, all surrounded by trees.

We found a spot on the grass to sit down, she'd been silent for a while and now she took both my hands, her eyebrows dipping as she looked at me.

"What's wrong?" I asked.

"Nothing ... just that I love you." She said with a sad expression.

"I love you too." It was the first time we'd said it but it didn't change the fact I was leaving tomorrow. "We've been putting this conversation off for too long."

She sniffed, "I'll really miss you, Dayna." A single tear rolled down her cheek, which I rubbed away with my thumb. "Please don't leave."

After a short silence, I looked at her and smiled. "How about I return after my exams?"

"Really?" Her face sprang to life. "For how long?"

"How about forever?" I said it more as a reflex but totally meant it, that I was asking to be in a relationship with Alessia. Not only that but I was willing to relocate to Italy to be with her and I knew the next words from her mouth would alter the entire course of my life.

She thought for a moment even as my heart pounded away in my chest, the silence pure agony.

"Dayna, that would make me the happiest girl in the world." She threw her arms around me and we collapsed to the floor in kisses.

I returned to England and even though I hated being away from my love, I kept my head down and studied for my exams. After a few weeks, Alessia told me how she'd informed her parents about us. Although at first Alberto was shocked, he admitted that deep down he already knew his daughter was a lesbian. He was indeed happy for us and was excited to be having me living back on the Villa di Giordano.

I received a degree in Italian language studies with first class honours and within two weeks I was back on a plane to Pisa, where Alessia was waiting. It'd been three months since we last saw each other and I was happy to see and feel that all our passion and lust still remained. When we embraced in *arrivals*, I knew that I never wanted to be apart from her ever again.

When we arrived at the Villa di Giordano, all I could think about was tearing off Alessia's clothes and spending the next few days in bed with her. Only, things didn't work out that way.

As the front door opened, we were greeted with a loud "*surprise!*" Then the lights turned on to reveal Marco, his new girlfriend and many of Alessia's friends I hadn't yet had the opportunity to meet. Alberto and Maria, as Alessia explained, had been kind enough to take a long needed skiing vacation in the Swiss Alps. It was torture having to entertain for several hours, Alessia outfitted in a tight fitting red cocktail dress and high heels that really pushed out her calves and for too long I had to watch her walking about, mingling with the guests, yes, she knew what she was doing to me, but God, I loved it, and by the time everybody left, I was ready to burst.

As soon as midnight arrived, I couldn't usher the guests out fast enough, whilst still trying to remain at least a little polite. And without any more words being spoken, I grabbed her hand and dragged her to our room, slamming the door shut.

We didn't emerge for a long time.

Novels

Euro Tripped

Where Are You

A Petal And A Thorn

Novellas

Trapped

Made in the USA
Monee, IL
24 December 2020

55521028R00066